The kiss came as such a shock that Shweta stood absolutely still for a few seconds.

The sensation was indescribable. She'd been kissed before, but the feel of Nikhil's warm, demanding lips on hers was something else altogether—involuntarily, she clutched at his arms, trying to pull him closer.

His hands were cupping her face now and with a little inarticulate cry, Shweta arched her body to lean in closer to the kiss. She was conscious of nothing other than the feel of Nikhil's lips on her mouth and throat.

A lot of time seemed to have gone by when Nikhil let her go finally, and she stared at him, her eyes still a little hazy from the effect of his kisses. One of his hands came to rest lightly on her shoulder, and the other caressed her cheek, as he ran a thumb gently over her lower lip.

"I should apologise," he said softly, and his voice was not quite steady. "I shouldn't have done that. But I'm not sorry I did."

Dear Reader,

This is my fourth book, and I started writing it almost immediately after I completed the third. I had the characters and plot ideas all mapped out in my head and for the first time in my short writing career I felt I'd got the 'hang' of writing—this book would be an absolute breeze. Of course when I started writing about Nikhil and Shweta, they took on a life of their own, deviating from my carefully planned plot at every possible opportunity (I hated it—I'm a control freak who only likes people who do as they're told!).

Shweta is attractive and outgoing, but she's been ruled by convention for most of her life, and is terribly risk averse. Nikhil on the other hand is the quintessential bad boy. He's strikingly good-looking, and while he's out of the rock bands and fast motorbikes phase, he's still a far cry from the nice, safely eligible kind of man Shweta is looking for.

Nikhil and Shweta were classmates from the ages of four to fourteen—they fought almost constantly, and if someone had told Shweta that she'd end up falling for Nikhil many years later, she'd have been horrified. Nikhil on the other hand always had a soft corner for her, and he finds the new, grown-up Shweta infinitely alluring. And in spite of my control freakiness, I found myself liking both of them more and more as they muddled their way towards admitting that they are crazily in love with each other.

Happy reading!

Shoma

THE ONE SHE WAS WARNED ABOUT

BY
SHOMA NARAYANAN

First published in Great Britain 2013
by Mills & Boon, an imprint of Harlequin (UK) Limited,
Harlequin (UK) Limited, Eton House, 18-24 Paradise Road,
Richmond, Surrey TW9 1SR

© Shoma Narayanan 2013

ISBN: 978 0 263 23586 9

Harlequin (UK) policy is to use papers that are natural, renewable and recyclable products and made from wood grown in sustainable forests. The logging and manufacturing processes conform to the legal environmental regulations of the country of origin.

Printed and bound in Great Britain
by CPI Antony Rowe, Chippenham, Wiltshire

Shoma Narayanan started reading Mills & Boon® romances at the age of eleven, borrowing them from neighbours and hiding them inside textbooks so that her parents didn't find out. At that time the thought of writing one herself never entered her head—she was convinced she wanted to be a teacher when she grew up. When she was a little older she decided to become an engineer instead, and took a degree in electronics and telecommunications. Then she thought a career in management was probably a better bet, and went off to do an MBA. That was a decision she never regretted, because she met the man of her dreams in the first year of business school—fifteen years later they're married with two adorable kids, whom they're raising with the same careful attention to detail that they gave their second-year project on organizational behaviour.

A couple of years ago Shoma took up writing as a hobby—after successively trying her hand at baking, sewing, knitting, crochet and patchwork—and was amazed at how much she enjoyed it. Now she works grimly at her banking job through the week, and tries to balance writing with household chores during weekends. Her family has been unfailingly supportive of her latest hobby, and are also secretly very, very relieved that they don't have to eat, wear or display the results!

To Anna and Megan, my two wonderful editors,
for their patience and unfailing support

CHAPTER ONE

'THAT,' PRIYA SAID, pointing dramatically, 'is the hottest man I have ever seen in my life.'

It was the first evening of their annual office convention and Shweta was already exhausted. The flight from Mumbai to Kerala was short, but it had been very early in the morning and she'd not slept much. Then the day had been crammed with intensely boring presentations that she'd had to sit through with a look of rapt attention on her face.

'At least look at him!' Priya was saying, and Shweta looked in the direction of her pointing finger.

A jolt of recognition made her keep staring for a few seconds, but there was no answering gleam in the man's eyes—clearly he didn't remember her at all. Not surprising, really. She'd changed quite a bit since they'd last met.

She shrugged, turning away. 'Not my type.'

Priya gave her a disbelieving stare. 'Delusional,' she said, shaking her head sadly. 'You're so out of touch with reality you can't tell a hot man from an Excel spreadsheet. Talking of spreadsheets—that's one guy I'd like to see spread on my sheets...'

Shweta groaned. 'Your sense of humour is pathetic,' she said. 'Every time I think you've reached rock-bottom you find a spade and begin to dig.'

Priya took a swig from her glass of almost-neat vodka. 'Yours isn't much better,' she pointed out. 'And, pathetic sense of humour or not, I at least have a boy-friend with a pulse. Unlike that complete no-hoper Sid-dhant...'

'Siddhant is not...' Shweta began to say, but Priya wasn't listening to her.

'Ooh, he's looking at you,' she said. 'I bet you can't get him to come and talk to you.'

'Probably not. I'm really not interested.' The man had given her a quick glance, his brows furrowed as he obviously tried to place her.

'You're a wuss.'

'This is childish.' She'd changed a lot since he'd last seen her—if he'd recognised her he'd have definitely come across.

'Bet you a thousand rupees.'

Shweta shrugged. 'Sorry, not enough. That pair of shoes I saw last week cost...'

'OK, five thousand!'

'Right, you're on,' Shweta said decisively.

The man across the room was looking at her again. Shweta took a comb and a pair of spectacles out of her purse. By touch she made a middle parting in her hair and, with little regard for the artfully careless style she'd spent hours achieving, braided it rapidly into two plaits.

Then she scrubbed the lipstick off her lips with a tissue and put on the spectacles. She still had her contact lenses in and the double vision correction made everything look blurry.

Even so, Priya's look of horror was unmistakable.

'What's wrong with you?' she hissed. 'You look like the Loch Ness monster. Where did you get those spectacles from? They're hideous!'

Shweta cut her off, nodding at the man, who was now purposefully headed in their direction. 'Mission accomplished,' she said, and Priya's jaw dropped.

She was still gaping at him as he came up to them. Close up, he was even more breathtaking—over six feet tall, and exuding an aura of pure masculinity that was overwhelming. He was looking right at Shweta, and the quirky, lopsided smile on his perfectly sculpted mouth made him practically irresistible.

'Shweta Mathur!' he said. 'My God, it's been years!'

He'd thought she looked familiar, but until she'd put on the spectacles he'd had no clue who she was. It was fifteen years since he'd seen her last—they'd been in middle school then, and if Shweta had been the stereotypical hard-working student, he'd been the stereotypical bad boy. He hadn't changed much, but Shweta had blossomed. She'd always had lovely eyes, and with the spectacles gone they were breathtaking, drawing you in till you felt you were drowning in them.... Nikhil shook himself a little, telling himself he was getting over-sentimental as he neared his thirtieth birthday. But the eyes were pretty amazing, even if you looked at them with a completely cynical eye. Her features were neat and regular, her skin was a lovely golden-brown, and even in her prim black trousers and top her figure looked pretty good. Somewhere along the line she'd even learnt how to use make-up—right now, in her bid to make him recognise her, she'd scrubbed off all her lipstick, and the vigorous treatment had made her un-expectedly lush lips turn a natural red.

'Hi, Nikhil,' Shweta said, holding her hand out primly.

Nikhil disregarded it, pulling her into his arms for a hug instead.

Shweta gave a little yelp of alarm. She'd recognised Nikhil the second she'd seen him—the slanting eye-brows and the hint of danger about him were pretty much the way they had been when they were both four-teen. But back then his shoulders hadn't been so broad, nor had his eyes sparkled with quite so much devilry. There was something incredibly erotic about the feel of his arms around her and the clean, masculine scent of his body. Shweta emerged from the hug consider-ably more flustered than before.

'You cheated!' Priya wailed. 'You crazy cow, you didn't tell me you *knew* him!'

Nikhil raised his eyebrows. 'Does it matter?'

Priya turned to him, eager to vent her ire on some-one. 'Of course it bloody does. You looked at her a cou-ple of times and I bet her five thousand she wouldn't be able to get you to come across and introduce your-self. She should have *said* she knew you.' She glared at Shweta. 'You're not getting that five grand.'

'Fine. And the next time your mother calls me to ask where you are I'll tell her the truth, shall I?'

Shweta and Priya shared a flat, and Shweta had spent the last six years making up increasingly inventive excuses to explain Priya's nights away from the flat every time her mother called to check on her.

Priya's eyes narrowed. 'Wait till I catch you alone,' she said, and flounced off in deep dudgeon.

Nikhil grinned and tweaked Shweta's hair as she shook it out of the braids. 'Still not learnt how to play nicely, have you?'

Oh, God, that took her back to her schooldays in an instant. And the feel of his hands in her hair... Shweta shook herself crossly. What was *wrong* with her? She had known Nikhil Nair since kindergarten, when both of them had been remarkably composed four-year-olds in a room full of bawling children. They'd grown up together, not always friends—in fact they'd fought almost constantly. A dim memory stirred of other girls sighing over him as they reached their teens, but she didn't remember thinking he was good-looking. Maybe she'd been a particularly unawakened fourteen-year-old. Looking at him now, she couldn't imagine how she had ever been impervious to him.

He was still laughing at her, and she tossed her head. 'And *you* are quite as annoying as you ever were,' she said, realising that she was willing him to comment on her hugely improved looks since the last time he'd seen her. He was looking at her intently, and as his gaze lingered around her mouth she wished she hadn't rubbed off the lipstick. She put up her hand self-consciously.

Given her general clumsiness, she'd probably smudged the stuff all over her face and now looked like Raju the circus clown.

He smiled slightly. 'It's all gone,' he said, and then, almost to himself, 'Little Shweta—who'd have thought it...? You're all grown-up now.'

'You haven't shrunk either,' she blurted out, and then blushed a fiery red.

Thankfully he didn't come back with a smart retort. 'I lost track of you after I left school,' he said instead, his eyes almost tender as they rested on her face.

Ha! Left school! He'd been expelled when the headmaster had found him smoking behind the school chapel.

'What have you been doing with yourself?'

'Nothing exciting,' she said 'College, then a chartered accountancy course. Shifted from Pune to Mumbai. And I've been working here ever since.' The 'here' was accompanied by a gesture towards the stage, where her firm's logo was prominently and tastelessly displayed. 'How about you? How come you're here?'

She didn't know everyone who worked in the firm—actually, she didn't know more than two or three of the people from the Delhi office—but she would have bet her last rupee that Nikhil hadn't buckled to convention and become an accountant. School gossip had pegged him as the boy most likely to become a millionaire—it had also estimated that he was the one most likely to go to jail. Not because he was a cheat or a thief, but he had always had a regrettable tendency to get into fist fights.

'I'm helping organise the convention for your firm,' he said.

Shweta looked surprised. 'You work with the event management company, then?' she asked. 'Leela Events?'

Nikhil nodded. 'Sort of,' he said.

Leela Events was big, and organised everything from Bollywood movie launches to corporate bashes. This was the first time her firm had engaged them, but she remembered the HR director saying that it had been quite a coup getting them in for a relatively small event.

The doors of the banquet hall opened and Nikhil touched her briefly on the arm. 'I'll catch up with you in a bit,' he said. 'I need to go and start earning my living.'

Shweta watched him go, her senses in turmoil. She had never been affected so strongly by a man, and even all the alarm bells clanging in her head weren't enough to stop her wanting to pull him back to her side.

'He *owns* Leela Events,' Priya said, reappearing by her side. 'Hot *and* loaded. If you're thinking of making a play for him, now's the time.'

Shweta turned away, coming abruptly back to earth. She should have guessed that Nikhil wouldn't be working for someone else. Owning a company at twenty-nine. Wow! So, definitely on the millionaire path, then—if he wasn't one already.

'I'm with Siddhant,' she said, her tone turning defensive as Priya raised an eyebrow. 'Well, kind of....'

Siddhant Desai was the youngest partner in the accounting firm Shweta worked for. They had been dating for a while, and things were on the verge of getting serious, though Siddhant hadn't actually popped the question yet.

'Don't marry him,' Priya said impulsively. 'He's beady-eyed and boring and he...' She wound to a stop as Shweta glared at her. 'He's just not right for you,' she said lamely.

'I don't want to discuss it,' Shweta snapped, but she had a niggling feeling that Priya was right. She'd never pretended even to herself that she was in love with Siddhant, but he was nice, her father would approve of him, and she'd thought that she could make it work. Of late, though, he'd begun to get on her nerves with his constant carping and complaining if things didn't go exactly as he'd planned.

'Talk of the devil...' Priya said, and made herself scarce as Siddhant came up to join Shweta.

He was good-looking in a conservative kind of way, and right now he was in an excellent mood. Shweta gave him a critical look. He was *safe*, she decided. That was what had drawn her to him. But safe could be boring sometimes....

'Sweetheart, you shouldn't be drinking that muck,' he said, smiling at Shweta and trying to take her glass away from her. 'Let me get you a proper drink.'

'Apple juice *is* a proper drink,' Shweta said, stubbornly holding on to her glass. She never drank at office parties—alcohol had the effect of disastrously loosening her tongue. There was a very real risk of her mortally offending a senior partner and finding herself without a job. 'Look, they're about to begin,' she said, pointing at the stage to distract Siddhant.

It was set up on one side of the banquet hall, and designed to look like a giant flatscreen TV. A rather over-enthusiastic ponytailed male MC was bouncing around exhorting people to come and take their places.

'I'm back,' Nikhil announced, materialising at her side so suddenly that Shweta jumped.

'I thought you'd gone off to earn your living,' she said.

'Just needed to do a quick check and see that everything's on track,' he replied. 'I have a relatively new team working on this event—good guys, but I thought I should be around in case something goes wrong.'

The team was still very raw, and normally he wouldn't have left their side for a moment—only he hadn't been able to keep himself away from Shweta. He tried to figure out why. While she'd metamorphosed into quite a stunner, he met equally good-looking girls every day in his chosen profession. It was the tantalising glimpses he could see of the gawky, independent-minded girl he'd known in school that drew him to her. He'd always liked her, in spite of the unmerciful teasing he'd subjected her to. At fourteen, though, he'd never consciously thought of her as a girl. Now it was impossible not to think of her as a woman, and the change was singularly appealing.

'You're not the nagging kind of boss, then?' Shweta asked.

It sounded as if she approved.

'You don't hover over your people telling them what to do and how to do it, when they should have it done…?'

Nikhil laughed. 'It's a little difficult to be like that in my business,' he said. 'There's a lot of planning involved, but people need the freedom to take spot decisions.'

Siddhant cleared his throat and Shweta realised guiltily that she'd completely forgotten he was standing next to her. Nikhil noticed him as well, giving him a friendly smile as he held out his hand.

'Nikhil Nair,' he said.

Siddhant took his hand, sounding almost effusive. 'Yes, of course. Manish mentioned you'd be here. I'm Siddhant.'

Priya had been right, then—Nikhil had to be loaded. Siddhant was this friendly only with the very successful or the very rich.

'You're one of the partners in the firm, aren't you?' Nikhil asked with a quick smile. 'I understand you guys are putting on a performance for the team?'

Oh, God. The firm's senior partner, Manish, had come up with the brilliant idea of all the partners dancing to a Bollywood number. On stage. Manish himself could dance well, though he was grossly overweight, most of the rest were terrible—and that was putting it mildly. Siddhant wasn't as bad as some, only he was very stiff and self-conscious. Shweta cringed at the thought of watching him make a fool of himself in public.

'It's just something Manish thought would make us seem a little more approachable to the team,' Siddhant was saying. 'That becomes a problem sometimes in an industry like ours. By the way—marvellous arrangements this morning. Your team did a fabulous job. The elephants and the Kathakali dancers welcoming everyone…and that flash mob thing at lunchtime was also a fantastic idea.'

The flash mob *had* been brilliant. Shweta conceded that much. But Siddhant was sounding a little sycophantic. Maybe Manish had asked him to make a pitch to Nikhil. She had only a vague idea of how event management companies operated, and it was unlikely Manish knew more than her—he usually operated on the principle that any company that made money needed accountants.

'Thank you,' Nikhil said, clearly amused. 'Can I borrow Shweta for a minute?'

Siddhant looked a bit taken aback, and Shweta hastened to explain. 'We were together in school—met again after years today.' *Borrow* her, indeed. He made her sound like a library book—and a not very interesting one at that.

'Oh, that's good,' Siddhant said. His eyes darted between the two of them as if he was registering for the first time that Nikhil could pose some kind of threat to his slow-paced courtship. 'But aren't you staying for the performances? I thought there were some Bollywood stars coming down…'

'Seen them many times before,' Nikhil said, a quick smile flashing across his face. 'I'll try and be back before you guys go on stage. Wouldn't want to miss that.'

He slung a casual arm around Shweta's shoulders as he drew her away and she felt her senses instantly go on high alert. He must have touched her in school, she thought, confused, but she didn't remember feeling anything like this—what was wrong with her? He'd changed, of course, but how had he turned from the wild tearaway schoolboy she remembered to someone who drove her crazy with longing without even trying—it was totally unfair.

'Is Siddhant your boss?' Nikhil asked once they were some distance away. When Shweta shook her head he said, 'Hmm…something going on between you guys, then? He looked quite possessive for a bit back there.'

'He's just a friend,' Shweta said, but the colour flaring up to her cheeks betrayed her yet again.

Nikhil grinned wickedly. 'Just a friend, eh? He's still looking at us. OK if I do this?' He bent his head and brushed his lips against her cheek. It was a fleeting caress, but Shweta felt her heart-rate triple.

Nikhil stepped back a little and gave her a considering look. 'Will he come charging up and challenge me to a duel?' he asked.

She shook her head mutely.

'OK—what if I do this?'

Shweta swatted his hands away as he brought them up to cup her face. Feeling all hot and bothered, she said, 'Stop playing the fool, Nikhil!'

He stepped back, raising his hands in laughing surrender. 'I've stopped…I've stopped. You're dangerous when you lose your temper—I don't want you giving me another scar.'

'Rubbish!' she said.

'Not at all.' Nikhil pushed his shaggy hair off his forehead with one hand and she saw it—a thin white scar across one temple that stood out against his tanned skin. 'The last time I annoyed you I ended up with this.'

Shweta remembered it quite vividly. She'd grabbed a wooden blackboard duster off the teacher's table and thrown it at him. But it still hadn't wiped the mocking grin off his face. A thin ribbon of blood had trickled down one side of his face and he'd mopped it off with a grimy handkerchief. He'd been laughing all the while. Right, so that was one time she remembered touching him—evidently he hadn't had the same effect on her then as he did now.

'I'm sorry,' she said awkwardly. In retrospect she was—a few centimetres the other way and she could have blinded him.

'It wasn't your fault,' he said. 'From what I remember I was quite an obnoxious little beast—you helped knock some sense into me. And every time I look in the mirror now I think of you....'

He lowered his voice to a sexy rasp for the last part of the sentence, and Shweta felt a visceral reaction kick in. It wasn't *fair*—he was just playing around without realising what he was doing to her. And with Siddhant watching...

Belatedly, she remembered Siddhant's existence, and turned around to look for him.

'Too late,' Nikhil said. 'He gave you a minute and then he went in, looking like a thundercloud. You'll have to grovel to get him to forgive you.'

'Fat chance,' Shweta said shortly.

Nikhil's accurate reading of Siddhant was unnerving, though. Right from when they'd first started dating

Siddhant had given the impression that he was assessing her against a set of strict criteria. Rather like the way he screened job applicants, actually. At all times she was conscious of his approval or disapproval. He rarely lost his temper, retiring instead into a stately silence that she had to coax him out of. Completely out of the blue she wondered what a relationship with Nikhil would be like. Unpredictable, definitely, but lively—she could imagine impassioned arguments followed by equally passionate reconciliations.

'Dreaming of something?' Nikhil asked teasingly.

Her eyes whipped back to him. She shook her head, trying to stop thinking of what a passionate reconciliation with him would be like.

'Look, are you really keen on watching the show? It'd be nice to catch up, but I'm leaving tomorrow morning. Want to sneak off with me somewhere?'

Oh, yes, she *did* want to sneak off with him. Put like that, it sounded deliciously wanton—also, no one had ever suggested sneaking off with her before.

Shweta tried not to look over-eager. 'I can slip away. I'm not terribly keen on the Bollywood dancers anyway.'

'Maybe you should tell Siddhant you're leaving,' Nikhil suggested.

But Shweta had decided to spend at least one evening free of his petty tyranny. 'He's not even my boss,' she said. 'I'll message Priya so that she doesn't get worried.'

It was only once they were in the black SUV that Nikhil had hired for the day that it occurred to Shweta to ask where they were going.

'It's a place where the locals hang out,' he said. 'Good music, and the food's to die for. Not too swanky. But we can go to one of the five-star hotels around here if you'd prefer that?'

'Yes—like I'd choose the five-star hotel after *that* introduction,' Shweta said. 'And you should know I'm not the swanky restaurant type.'

'You might have changed,' Nikhil said. 'You don't look the same—for all I know you might have turned into a wine-sipping socialite, scorning us lesser mortals…'

Shweta punched him in the arm and he laughed. 'Still violent, I see,' he said, but his tone was more tender than mocking. She felt her heart do an obedient little flip-flop in response. At least now her reactions to him weren't coming as a surprise. All she had to do was work harder at concealing them.

They were on the outskirts of the city now, and driving down a narrow lane flanked by fields and coconut trees.

'OK if I roll down the window?' Nikhil asked.

When she nodded, he switched off the air-conditioning and got the windows down.

'We're lucky it's not raining,' he said. 'Kerala gets most of its rains in winter…'

'I know. I used to pay attention in Geography,' Shweta said pertly. 'Unlike you.'

Nikhil gave her a mocking smile. 'You were such a *gooooood* little girl,' he said, dragging his words out. 'Of *course* you paid attention.'

Shweta carefully controlled an urge to hit him on

the head with a high-heeled shoe. 'And you were such a *baaad* boy.' She copied his tone as closely as she could. 'Of *course* you paid attention to no one and were good for nothing.'

'Bad boys are good at some things,' he murmured suggestively.

Shweta flushed as all the things he was probably very, very good at sprang to mind. God, was he doing it on purpose? Probably he thought it was fun, getting her all hot and bothered. There was no way he could be actually flirting with her—or was he?

'Do you know where you're going?' she asked in her best auditor voice—the one that Priya swore made entire finance departments quake in their shoes.

Nikhil nodded. 'Almost there.'

The road had developed some rather alarming twists and turns, and he was concentrating on his driving. In Shweta's opinion he was going too fast, but she'd boil her favourite shoes in oil before she said anything—there was no point giving him an opportunity to make remarks about fraidy-cat accountants. She fixed her eyes on Nikhil instead, hoping the man would take her mind off his driving. It worked. The moonlight illuminated his rather stern profile perfectly, throwing the planes and angles of his face into relief.

He was really quite remarkably good-looking, Shweta thought. It was a wonder she hadn't noticed it in school, but she had an explanation. In those days she'd been completely obsessed by a rather chocolate-faced movie star, and had unconsciously compared everyone she saw with him. Nikhil was the complete oppo-

site of chocolate-faced—even at fourteen his features
had been uncompromisingly male. Her eyes drifted
towards his shoulders and upper body, and then to his
hands on the steering wheel. He had rather nice hands,
she thought, strong with square-tipped fingers. Unbidden, she started to wonder how those hands would feel
on her body, and she blushed for probably the twelfth
time that evening.

The car negotiated a final hairpin bend, after which
the road seemed to shake itself out and lose steam. It
went on for a couple of hundred metres through a rather
dense copse of coconut trees and ended abruptly on a
beach.

'Are you lost?' she enquired. He shook his head.
'Come on,' he said, opening his door and leaping down
lightly.

He was at her door and handing her down before she
could protest. Locking the car with a click of the remote, he put an arm around her shoulders and started
walking her to the beach.

Their destination was a small, brightly lit shack
thatched with palm fronds. There were small tables
laid out in front, some of which were occupied by locals. Nikhil chose a table with a view of the beach. The
moon had risen now, and the sea had a picture-postcard
quality to it. A motherly-looking woman in her fifties
bustled out, beaming in delight when she saw Nikhil.
She greeted him in a flood of Malayalam which Shweta
didn't even bother trying to follow. She wasn't particularly good at languages, and Malayalam was nothing
like Hindi or any other language she knew.

'Meet Mariamma,' Nikhil said. 'She's known me since I was a kid.'

Shweta smiled and Mariamma switched to heavily accented English. 'Am always happy to meet Nikhil's friends,' she said, dispelling any notion that this was the first time Nikhil had brought someone here with him. 'Miss Shweta, do sit down. I'll get you a menu.'

'I thought you didn't have one?' Nikhil murmured.

Mariamma said chidingly, 'You haven't been in touch for a long while. We got a menu printed—Jossy designed it on his laptop.'

'I'd love to see it, but I know what I want to order,' Nikhil said. 'Shweta, any preferences?'

'If you could order for me...' Shweta said, and Nikhil promptly switched back into Malayalam and reeled off a list of stuff that sounded as if it would be enough to feed the entire state for a week.

Mariamma beamed at both of them and headed back to the kitchen, her cotton sari rustling as she left.

'You come here often?'

'I used to—when I was a child. My grandparents lived quite near here, and Mariamma was one of my aunt's closest friends.'

'Your grandparents...?'

'Died when I was in college.'

Nikhil was frowning, and Shweta wished she hadn't asked.

'Are you in touch with anyone from our class in school?' she asked hastily.

He began to laugh. 'You need to be more subtle when you're changing the topic,' he said. 'No. I e-mail some of my old crowd on and off, but I haven't met up with anyone for a long while. Ajay and Wilson are in the States now, and Vineet's building a hotel in Dehra Dun. How about you?'

'I'm not building a hotel in Dehra Dun,' Shweta said, and made a face. 'I'm in touch with Vineet too. He's difficult to avoid. And a couple of other people as well.'

'Have they got used to your new avatar?' He was still finding it difficult to reconcile Shweta who looked like a million bucks but sounded like the old tomboyish Shweta he'd known for most of his adolescent years.

Shweta frowned at him. 'What avatar?'

'I remember you as a serious, pigtailed little thing, very grim and earnest all the time—except when you were climbing trees and challenging me to cycling races.'

'And now?'

'And now…' He smiled and leaned back in his chair. 'Well, you've chosen a grim and serious profession, all right, but in spite of that…something's changed. You've been rebelling, haven't you? You look different, of course, but that's just the contact lenses and the new hairstyle.'

A little piqued at his dismissal of the change in her looks, she said firmly, 'Well, I haven't been rebelling.'

'Sure?' he asked teasingly. 'You came away with me instead of staying back with that extremely eligible, extremely boring young man.'

'I haven't seen you for fifteen years,' she pointed out. 'I see Siddhant every day.'

'And your shoes…'

She looked down at them defensively. They *were* rather lovely shoes—high-heeled green pumps that struck a bright note against her sombre black trousers and top. She was wearing a silver hand-crafted necklace studded with peridots—the stones perfectly matched the shoes. In spite of having read a dozen articles that condemned matching accessories as the height of uncool, she found it difficult to stop herself, especially when it came to shoes. Speaking of which...

'What's wrong with my shoes?'

'Nothing,' he said, looking amused. 'They're...very striking, that's all. But otherwise you're very conservatively dressed.' Before she could protest, he said, 'Sorry, I've been reading too many articles on pop psychology. But I stick by what I say—it's a slow rebellion, but you're rebelling all the same. I always thought your father was way too strict with you.'

'I've been living away from home for over seven years,' Shweta said indignantly. 'All my rebelling is long over and done with. And he's changed. He's not the way he used to be.' Her father had been a bit of a terror when she was younger, and most of her classmates had given him a wide berth. It had taken Shweta herself years to muster up the courage to stand up to him.

'If you say so.' Somehow seeing Shweta again had brought out the old desire in Nikhil to wind her up, watch her struggle to control her temper—except she was now all grown up, and instead of wanting to tug her pigtails and trip her over during PE class he wanted to reach out and touch her, to run his hands over her smooth skin and tangle them in her silken hair...

Realising that his thoughts were wandering a bit too far, he picked up the menu and started leafing through it. A thought struck him. 'You haven't turned vegetarian, have you?'

He looked relieved when Shweta shook her head. 'Thank heavens. I've ordered mutton stew and appams and prawn curry—I just assumed you'd be OK with all of it.'

'Of course I am. I've always loved prawn curry. Your mom used to cook it really well, I remember.'

'Which mom?' he asked, his mouth twisting into a wry smile.

Shweta felt like kicking herself. Nikhil was illegitimate, and had always been touchy about his family. His father had taken a mistress after ten years of a childless marriage, scandalising everyone who knew him, and Nikhil was his mistress's son. Perhaps it would have been less scandalous if he'd tried to keep the affair secret, but when he'd found out that Ranjini was pregnant he'd brought her to live in the same house as his wife. Until he was four Nikhil had thought having two mothers was a perfectly normal arrangement—it was only when he joined school that he realised he lived in a very peculiar household.

'Veena Aunty,' Shweta said.

Veena was Nikhil's father's wife. If they'd been Muslims Nikhil's father could have taken a second wife, but as a Hindu he would have been committing bigamy if he'd married Ranjini. Veena had taken the whole thing surprisingly well. People had expected her to resent Ranjini terribly, even if she couldn't do anything about

having to share a house with her, but Veena appeared
to be on quite good terms with her. And she adored
Nikhil, which perhaps wasn't so surprising given that
she didn't have children of her own. In his teen years
at least Nikhil had been equally attached to her—all
his sullenness and resentment had been directed towards his parents.

'How're they doing?' Shweta asked. 'Your parents, I
mean.' She'd met them only a few times—her father had
made sure that she didn't have much to do with Nikhil.

Nikhil shrugged. 'OK, I guess. I haven't seen them
for over four years.'

Shweta's eyebrows shot up. 'Aren't they still in Pune,
then?'

'Dad has some property in Trivandrum. They moved
there when Dad retired. They're still there—though
now Amma is pretending to be a cousin and Mom tells
everyone that she's married to Dad.'

The words came out easily enough, but Shweta
could see his jaw tense up and was very tempted to
lean across the table and take his hand, smooth away
the frown lines. He'd always called his own mother
Mom, while his father's wife went by the more affectionate Amma.

'I guess it's easier that way,' Shweta said. 'Rather
than having to explain everything to a whole new set
of people.'

'Pity they didn't think of it when it really mattered.'
His voice was tight, almost brittle. 'I don't know why
Amma is letting them do this.'

'I'm sure she has her reasons. Maybe you could visit

them now that you're already in Kerala?' Shweta believed strongly in women standing up for themselves—
in her view Veena was quite as responsible for the
situation as Nikhil's parents.

'Not enough time—I've got to be back in Mumbai
for another gig. Plus I'm not on the best of terms right
now with my father.' He was still frowning, but after a
few seconds he made a visible effort to smile. 'While
we're on the subject of parents, how're your dad and
aunt?'

'He's retired, so now he bosses the gardener and the
cleaners around instead of his patients,' Shweta said,
and Nikhil laughed.

Shweta's father had been a doctor in a fairly well-
known hospital in Pune, and he'd inspired a healthy
respect in everyone who knew him. Shweta's mother
had died quite suddenly of a heart attack when Shweta
was three, and her father's unmarried older sister had
moved in to help bring up Shweta.

'And your aunt?'

'She's still keeping house for him. Though she grum-
bles about him to whoever's willing to listen—wonders
how my mother put up with him for so many years.'

A lot of people had wondered that, but Nikhil didn't
say so. He'd met Shweta's father several times—he'd
been on their school board, and had chaired the disciplinary hearing that had led to his final expulsion
from the school. Nikhil didn't hold that against him.
He'd been on a short wicket in any case, given that the
smoking incident had followed hard upon his having
'borrowed' their Hindi teacher's motorbike and taken

his best buddies out for a spin on it. But he had re-sented Dr Mathur telling Shweta not to have anything to do with him.

The food arrived and Mariamma came across to ladle generous portions onto their plates. 'Eat well, now,' she admonished Shweta. 'You're so thin—you girls nowadays are always on some diet or the other.'

'I can't diet to save my life,' Shweta said. 'I'm thin because I swim a lot.'

Mariamma sniffed disapprovingly, but Nikhil found it refreshing, being with a woman who wasn't obsessed with her figure. His job brought him into contact with models and actresses, all of whom seemed to be afraid to breathe in case the air contained calories. In his view Shweta had a better figure than all of them—she was slim, but not stick-thin, and her body curved nicely in all the right places.

'Like the food?' he asked, watching her as she dipped an *appam* into the curry and ate it with evident enjoyment. For a few seconds he couldn't take his eyes off her lush mouth as she ran her tongue over her bottom lip—the gesture was so innocently sexy.

'It's good,' she pronounced.

He dragged his eyes away from her face to concentrate on his own untouched plate before she could catch him staring.

'Everything's cooked in coconut oil, isn't it? It adds an interesting flavour to the food.'

Nikhil thought back to the last time he'd taken a girl on a date to a restaurant in Mumbai that served authentic Kerala cuisine. She'd hardly eaten anything, insisting that the food smelt like hair oil. She'd been annoying in many other ways as well, he remembered. Rude to waiters and refusing to walk even a few metres to the car because the pavement looked 'mucky'. Not for the first time he wondered why he chose to waste his time with empty-headed women like her rather than someone like Shweta. He didn't want to delve too deeply into the reasons, though—self-analysis wasn't one of his passions.

'Can I ask you something?' Shweta said as she polished off her last appam. 'Why were you out to get me in school? We used to be good friends when we were really little—till you began hanging out only with the boys and ignored me completely. And when we were twelve or something you started being really horrible. You used to be rude about my clothes and my hair-style—pretty much everything.'

'Was I that bad?' Nikhil looked genuinely puzzled. 'I remember teasing you a little, but it was light-hearted stuff. I didn't mean to upset you. Maybe it was because you were such a *good* little girl—listening to what the teacher said, doing your homework on time, never playing truant… It was *stressful*, studying with you. You set such high standards…'

He ducked as Shweta swatted at him with a ladle. 'Careful,' he said, his voice brimming over with laughter as drops of curry sprayed around. 'I don't want to go back looking like I've been in a food fight.'

'Oh, God—and your clothes probably cost a bomb, didn't they.' Conscience-stricken, Shweta put the ladle down. 'Did I get any on you?'

Nikhil shook his head. 'I don't think so. If I find any stains I'll send you the dry-cleaning bill.'

She looked up swiftly, wondering whether he was being serious, but the lurking smile in his eyes betrayed him. 'Oh, you wretch,' she scolded. 'I've a good mind to throw the entire dish at you.'

'Mariamma will be really offended,' he said gravely. 'And if you throw things at me I won't buy you dessert.'

'Oh, well that settles it, then. I'll be nice to you.' He hadn't really answered her question, but she didn't want to destroy the light-hearted atmosphere by pressing too hard. 'But only till we're done with dessert.'

CHAPTER TWO

'AREN'T YOU GOING to wear something under that? A *churidaar* or leggings?'

'It's a dress, Siddhant,' Shweta explained patiently. 'It's supposed to be worn like this.' Dresses had come back into fashion a couple of years ago, but evidently no one had informed Siddhant.

'I like you better in *salwar kameez*,' he said. 'Or even jeans. You look—I don't know—sort of weird in this. And the shoes…'

Shweta surveyed herself in the huge mirror in the hotel foyer. The simple pale yellow cotton dress set off her golden-brown skin and lovely black eyes to perfection. And the shoes were her favourite ones—flat open-toed white sandals with huge yellow cloth flowers on the straps. The flowers were even of the same genus/sub-species as the white printed ones on her dress, and until she'd come downstairs she'd been pretty happy with the overall effect.

During her childhood she'd been forced to wear truly horrible clothes—her aunt had had absolutely no sense of colour or style, and had usually bought Shweta's clothes at discount stores or got them made up by the local tailor. It didn't help that the tailor was the same one who'd made Dr Mathur's shirts. All her clothes had ended up with boxy cuts and mannish collars. She'd tried complaining to her father, but he'd told her she shouldn't be bothering about something as frivolous as clothes, and she'd been too much in awe of him to protest. It had only been when she was in college that she'd started choosing her own clothes and, while she knew her taste wasn't perfect, she hated anyone criticising what she wore.

'They're very nice shoes,' she told Siddhant firmly. 'Actually, all in all, I think I look pretty good.'

'I agree,' a voice said behind her.

She spun around to meet Nikhil's smiling eyes. Brilliant—now he probably thought she was needy and totally hungry for reassurance.

'I wasn't intending to criticise your clothes,' Siddhant said, after nodding stiffly to Nikhil. 'I just thought that jeans might be more practical, given that we're going sightseeing.'

He himself was dressed in khaki trousers and a crisp white short-sleeved shirt. Somehow, though, he managed to look a little stiff-necked and conservative next to Nikhil's rugged good looks.

Nikhil gave him an easy smile. 'We're driving to the backwaters and we'll spend the next few hours on a boat. It's hardly a Himalayan trek. Shweta—I came to ask you... You said you wanted to pick up some spices for your aunt, right? I've decided to stay back for another day, and I'll be taking the SUV out again—

you can ride with me. We'll stop at a spice garden I know—you'll get much better stuff there than you do in the stores.'

Shweta nodded happily. The alternative was to ride in a bus with the rest of the office crowd. Siddhant would be with the other partners in a specially rented van. Not that they were trying to be elitist, as he'd hastily clarified, but they had some urgent business to discuss, which was confidential, and it would be a pity to waste the travel time when all of them were together anyway.

He didn't look at all happy about Shweta going off with Nikhil, but there was little he could do about it. 'I'll see you at the boats, then,' he said.

'Yes, we should be there in a couple of hours,' Nikhil said. 'Come on, Shweta, we should leave now. See you in a bit, Siddhant. I was taking a look at the video of yesterday's dance, by the way—not bad at all. I wish I could have made it back in time for the actual performance.'

'Don't make fun of him,' Shweta said in an undertone as they waited for the car. 'He was pretty uncomfortable with this whole dance thing, but it was his boss's idea and he couldn't wriggle out of it.'

There was genuine surprise on Nikhil's face as he replied. 'I wasn't. OK, he isn't India's answer to Michael Jackson, but he did a good job. Must have practised a lot.'

'He's a bit of a perfectionist,' Shweta muttered.

She still hadn't figured Nikhil out. Maybe he'd been telling the truth the night before—he'd only been teasing her back then in school and she'd overreacted. An incipient persecution complex—that was what her father would call it.

'So is it serious, then?' Nikhil asked after a pause.

'With Siddhant? I don't know—we've not talked about it. We've been dating for a while, so I guess there's a good chance of us ending up together.'

'Are you in love with him?'

Startled, she felt her gaze fly up to his face. 'With Siddhant?' she asked again, stupidly.

He smiled. 'No, with that traffic policeman over there. Of course with Siddhant, you dimwit.'

'No,' she said, and then bit her lip. Impulsive frankness was all very well, but sometimes she wished she had more control over her tongue. 'I mean, I'm very fond of him, but it's a little too early. We've not actually...' Her voice trailed off as he began to smile. She must be sounding like an utter idiot to him. He'd already made it pretty clear that he didn't have a very high opinion of Siddhant, and her dithering was probably amusing him no end. Rapidly she moved the battle into enemy territory. 'What about you?' she asked. 'Are you in love with...well, whoever people might *think* you're in love with?'

'No, I'm not,' he said, his lips twitching.

A valet brought his black SUV around and Nikhil helped her in before heading around to the driver's side. The powerful engine purred to life as he turned the key in the ignition, but to her surprise he didn't start driving right away. Instead he was looking at her, his expression unfathomable.

'How keen are you on this spice-buying thing?'

'It's one of the must-dos if you're in Kerala, isn't it? Why? Is there a problem?'

'Well, the proper spice gardens are up in the hills,' he said. 'It's just that we had a good time yesterday—or at least I did—and I thought it would be good to hang out for a while without the rest of your group.'

Shweta took a few seconds to digest this. On the one hand there was something incredibly flattering about Nikhil wanting to spend more time with her. On the other the thought of slipping away for a clandestine rendezvous was a little unsettling. She hadn't got over her crush on Nikhil. If anything it was worse today— her stomach was going quivery just from her looking at him. Telling her stomach firmly to behave itself, she frowned at Nikhil.

'So there isn't a spice garden here at all?'

'There is.' Nikhil's smile was self-deprecatory. 'We can go there if you really want. Or we can go directly to the backwaters.'

'But we'll get there a lot earlier than the others,' Shweta pointed out. 'They haven't even started getting into the buses, and you drive like a maniac—you'll take half the time they will.'

'We'll take one of the small houseboats out,' he said. 'Just the two of us. It'll be more peaceful than joining a hundred accountants.'

'You really don't like accountants, do you?'

'I like some.'

His smile deepened as he looked right into her eyes,

and Shweta said hurriedly, 'OK, we'll take the boat,' before she could start blushing again.

Only later did she realise that he hadn't asked her if she wanted to come with him—he'd just assumed she would.

Once they reached the pier Shweta was glad Nikhil had made the choice for her. The small boat he was pointing out was a hundred times more charming than the double-decker monstrosities that were lined up for the rest of the group. And the backwaters were lovely—a network of canals opening into a huge, still expanse of water flanked by rows and rows of coconut trees. Little houseboats were moored by the banks, and there were water birds all around, gracefully swooping through the air to land on the water.

'Time slows down here,' Shweta said wonderingly as their boat was cast off and negotiated through one of the narrow channels into a wider stretch. 'It seems so far away from Mumbai.'

'It *is* pretty far from Mumbai.' There was a smile twitching at Nikhil's lips. 'Almost two thousand kilometres. But I know what you mean.'

'And people actually live in these boats?'

'These ones are mainly for the use of tourists,' he said. 'Take a look at the inside, if you want.'

The inside wasn't really all that impressive—it was just a small room with cane furniture, and in spite of the slow speed they had to be careful not to rock the boat by moving around it too much. And the bed in the centre was all too suggestive.

Suddenly very conscious that she was alone with Nikhil, Shweta said, 'It was nicer outside, wasn't it?'

'This isn't bad either,' Nikhil said. He was sprawled lazily on a cane chair, with a beer in one hand. 'Stop hopping around like a jittery kitten and sit down. I don't bite.'

'I should have brought my work phone,' Shweta said. 'There's an e-mail that's supposed to come in this morning from a client and I totally forgot.' She looked fretfully at her little yellow clutch purse. 'It wouldn't fit properly into this.' But the purse had perfectly matched her outfit, and she'd decided to leave her phone behind.

'You work very hard, don't you?'

It didn't sound as if he meant it as a compliment, and Shweta immediately went on the defensive. 'I don't work any harder than my colleagues do.'

'Nothing wrong with working hard,' he said. 'It's just that you don't seem to take any time out to have *fun*.'

He stretched out the word a little, and it was quite evident what kind of fun he had in mind. Despite herself, Shweta felt her cheeks growing warm.

'Don't make assumptions,' she snapped. 'I have enough fun, thank you very much. I needed to reply to this e-mail as soon as it comes in—that's why I'm worried.'

Nikhil got up and came to stand behind her. 'Do you want to go back?' he asked. 'We can if it's really urgent.'

For a second Shweta almost said yes. Not because the e-mail was all that urgent, but because Nikhil's proximity was throwing her nicely ordered world into turmoil. Then the ridiculousness of it all struck her and she shook her head.

'I'll phone him,' she said. 'It's just that this particular client is a bit picky—he calls up my boss for the smallest thing.'

As it turned out, though, the client was on a camping trip in Alibagh and had completely forgotten to send the e-mail before he left. He even had the grace to apologise for the delay.

'So that's OK, then,' she said after she rang off. 'I hate having work stuff hanging over me like that.'

'Stop thinking about work now,' Nikhil said, putting his hands on her shoulders.

Shweta went completely still as he started massaging her neck and shoulders gently. She could feel the tension seep out, but it was replaced by a set of entirely different sensations. She was acutely conscious of the strength in his lean hands. The temptation to turn into his arms was intense, and she felt positively bereft when he removed his hands after a few minutes.

'Why were you asking me about Siddhant?'

There was a little pause, then Nikhil said, 'I have a theory about the two of you. Look, I'm sorry—it's none of my business really.'

Of course as soon as he said that she *had* to know more.

'A theory about us?' she asked, trying to sound casual and unconcerned. Somehow, she had a feeling she wasn't fooling Nikhil one bit.

'You don't give a damn for him,' Nikhil said bluntly.

'But for some reason you've led him on to think that you're interested.'

Shweta flushed. Nikhil was only saying something Priya had been telling her for months, and there was no earthly reason she should feel the need to justify herself. She still found herself explaining, though.

'We've been dating for a while,' she said. 'I was planning to say yes if he asked me to marry him. It's only for the last month or so that I've not been so sure.'

'Why not?' he asked, his voice quiet.

Shweta felt that a lot depended on her answer. 'He's a little…' She'd been about to say *judgemental*, but it felt disloyal to be talking about Siddhant with Nikhil. 'I don't know what it is, really, but I don't think we'd suit.'

'You wouldn't.'

Her eyes widened at the bald statement. 'You hardly know either of us!' she said, and continued hastily when he raised his eyebrows, 'You knew me a long while ago. I was just a kid then. I've changed!'

'I'm sure you have,' Nikhil said. 'But you used to be a very straightforward person, and people don't change fundamentally. So what I find difficult to understand is why you'd even contemplate marrying a man you don't care two hoots about.'

Shweta glared at him. 'You just said it isn't any of your business, and I wholeheartedly agree,' she said. 'Why are you so bothered about me and Siddhant, anyway?'

'Because I don't want to feel guilty when I do this,' Nikhil said, bringing his head down to hers and kissing her mouth very, very gently.

Shweta stood stock-still, frozen in shock. A kiss was the last thing she'd been expecting, but the sensation was incredible, his lips warm and teasing against hers. Her hands came up involuntarily to clasp him around the neck. Oh, but it felt so good—familiar, and wildly exciting at the same time. She clung to him as the kiss deepened, giving a little gasp of protest when he finally stepped back.

'I've wanted to kiss you ever since I saw you yesterday,' he said, the edges of his voice rough with desire. 'It was all I could do to keep my hands off you.'

Shweta looked up at him, too shaken to speak. The kiss had awakened a swarm of emotions in her and she wasn't sure how to react.

Nikhil gazed back at her, his dark eyes smouldering. It was taking all his self-control not to pull her back into his arms. Her inexperience showed, though, and until he was sure of his own feelings he didn't want to go too far.

'Maybe we should go back outside,' he said, his voice softening as he put up a hand to touch her cheek. 'I don't trust myself alone with you for too long.'

Shweta felt like crying out in frustration. She *wanted* to be alone with him, to take the kiss further—but she could hardly say so. Mutely she followed him out on to the deck of the boat.

'The others should be on the boats by now,' he said. 'Do you want to wait till they catch up with us or go on to the village?'

'Go on to the village,' she muttered.

The last thing she wanted was a bunch of her colleagues gawking at her—Priya at least would be sure to smell a rat. And Siddhant... She needed to make it clear to him that it was off between them. Only it would be a slightly difficult thing to put across, given that he hadn't formally proposed in the first place.

Nikhil came to stand next to her, his sleeve brushing her bare arm as he leaned against the handrail. 'The boatman says we'll reach it in fifteen minutes,' he said. 'We'll get some time to look around the village then.'

Except that they didn't, because his new team head who was supposed to be managing the project had a sudden attack of nerves and Nikhil had to step in to avoid a crisis.

Left to her own devices, Shweta wandered around the little resort village, admiring the local handicrafts and watching a troupe of dancers rehearse their steps.

'Nikhil Sir is calling you,' one of the trainees said behind her, and Shweta turned to see Nikhil beckoning to her from the pier.

'The boats are about to come in,' he said as she joined him. 'We have a little surprise planned.'

He slung an arm casually around her shoulders and she had to fight the impulse to lean closer into his embrace. 'What kind of surprise?'

'Look,' he said.

The four large boats carrying the office gang were now lined up on either side of the narrow stretch of water.

'Aren't they docking?' she asked, puzzled. The boats seemed to be waiting for something. Before Nikhil could answer her, she realised what they were waiting for. 'The snake boats!' she said. 'But how's that possible...? This isn't the time of year for the races, is it?'

But the snake boats were there—immensely long canoes, with almost a hundred rowers per boat wearing T-shirts in their team colours over *veshtis*.

Shweta clutched at Nikhil's arm in excitement. 'I've always wanted to see the races!' she said. 'I used to watch them on TV when I was a kid, but this is the first time I've been to Kerala... Ooh, they're off!'

Nikhil smiled down at her, amused by her evident excitement. The snake boats *were* a pretty amazing sight. The teams of rowers, working in perfect synchronization, propelled them down the channel faster than the average motorboat. He was about to point out the finer points of the race when something caught his eye.

'Damn,' he muttered. Releasing Shweta's arm, he sprinted to the makeshift dais at the end of the pier which his team was using to make announcements from. The girl he'd put in charge was holding the microphone idly, her entire attention focussed on the snake boats.

Nikhil grabbed the mike from her. 'Viewing boat Number Two—yes, you guys on my left—please don't crowd near the guardrail. Your boat is tilting. We don't want you to land up in the water. Especially since I see that many of you have taken off your life jackets.'

There were some squeals of alarm from the occupants of the boat and they stepped back from the rail. The boat was still tilting a little, though not at quite such an alarming angle. Nikhil cast a quick eye around the other boats.

'Keep an eye on them,' he instructed, handing the mike back to his hugely embarrassed event manager. 'Don't panic them, but make sure the boat doesn't go over. And once everyone's on land call for a quick team meeting—this shouldn't have happened.'

'It wasn't her fault,' Shweta protested as Nikhil re-joined her. 'How was she to know that everyone would go thronging to one side?'

'It's her job to know,' he said, frowning. He'd been so distracted by Shweta that he'd lost sight of why he was really here. He should be with his team, making sure that nothing went wrong, but he hadn't been able to tear himself away from her side.

She was leaning forward a little now, her lips slightly parted as she watched the rowers put in a last furious effort to get the snake boats across the finish line.

'I knew the purple team would win,' she said, her eyes glowing with satisfaction.

Nikhil wished he could pull her into his arms and kiss her. Instead, he put a casual arm around her shoulders, pretending not to notice the slight quiver that ran through her. 'There's still one more race to go,' he said. 'I bet the yellow T-shirts win this time.'

'Purple,' she said, aware that she sounded a little breathless. Nikhil's proximity was doing strange things to her pulse-rate.

'Dinner with me in Mumbai if yellow wins?' he said.

Shweta looked up at him. 'And if they lose?'

'If they lose I'll take you out for dinner before we leave Kerala.'

'A little illogical, that.'

'Not really,' he said, and his voice was like a caress.

Shweta acted as if she hadn't heard him. Flirting was not something she was good at, and she suspected that Nikhil was only flirting with her out of habit. She knew she hadn't changed all that much from her schooldays—her glasses were gone, and she had a better hairstyle, but inside she was still the studious, slightly tomboyish and totally uncool girl she'd been fourteen years ago. The kiss she couldn't explain away. It had felt as if the attraction was as red-hot on his side as hers, but he'd pulled away and hadn't tried to get her alone afterwards. Of course they'd been under the gaze of his entire events crew—not to mention four boatloads of her colleagues.

'Watch,' he said as the snake boats lined up for the race.

Shweta dutifully turned her eyes in the direction he was pointing. His arm was still around her, and she found it difficult to concentrate on the race. Except for the frazzled girl with the mike no one else seemed to share her problem—even the waiters and performers were crowding onto the landing stage to watch the race. As for her colleagues on the boats—they were going crazy, whooping and blowing paper trumpets, though this time they were careful to stay away from the guardrail.

The yellow team won by a few metres and Shweta exhaled noisily.

'Dinner in Mumbai,' Nikhil said, looking down at her. 'I'll let you go back to your colleagues for today, then.'

Was that a dismissal? It didn't feel like one, and the thought that he'd be in touch when they returned to Mumbai made her pulse race a little faster.

'Pretty impressive, Mr Nair,' a voice said near them.

Anjalika Arora was one of the Bollywood entertainers who'd performed for the team the day before. In her late thirties, she was still strikingly beautiful. She'd never really made it to the top in films—the few in which she'd played the female lead had flopped dismally at the box office, and over the last few years she'd appeared in glitzy productions with all-star casts where she'd been only one of four or five glamorous leading ladies with very little to do. The gossip magazines said that she made a fortune in stage shows, dancing to the songs from those movies.

Shweta looked at her curiously. This was the first time she'd met even a minor celebrity face-to-face. Anjalika looked like anyone else, only a lot prettier— dressed as she was today, in denim cut-offs and a T-shirt, and with her hair tied up, she could have been a soccer mom, dropping her kid off for a game. Shweta tried to remember if she had children or not. Unfortunately the financial newspapers she took didn't say much about the private lives of movie stars. She did remember picking up a magazine at the beauty parlour which had covered a high-profile reconciliation between Anjalika and her movie producer husband.

'How was your morning?' Nikhil asked, releasing Shweta as Anjalika gave him a socialite-type kiss on the cheek.

'Oh, brilliant—I spent most of it in the spa,' Anjalika said, giving Shweta a girl-to-girl smile. 'It's pretty good—have you been there?' Before Shweta could respond she'd turned back to Nikhil. 'Nikhil, I hate to bother you while you're working, but I'm sure your amazing team can handle things. I have this teeny query which I need your help on...'

'Yes, of course.' Nikhil smiled at Shweta. 'I'll be back in half an hour, OK?'

Shweta nodded, and Anjalika gave her another brilliant smile before hooking an arm through Nikhil's and drawing him away.

'Wants a pay-hike, does she?' one of Nikhil's crew members muttered to another.

The man he was speaking to shrugged. 'It's standard practice for her. She waits till the event's underway and then starts haggling for more money. I don't think Nikhil will buckle, though—he'll sympathise, and say he'll do what he can, but she'll be lucky if he gives her even a rupee more than was actually agreed.'

'Or maybe he'll pay her in kind,' the first man said in an undertone. 'Take her back to the hotel and sweeten her up a bit. She must be gasping for it—her husband's got a floozy on the side, and she isn't as young as she used to be.'

'Yeah, and *he's* hot stuff with the women. That's how he gets some of these star types to come in for the smaller events—gives them a good time in bed and they're ready to do anything for him. Then, once the event's done with, he's off.'

'OK—minds out of the gutter, please, and back to work.'

Nikhil's second-in-command, a hearty-looking lady called Payal, strode up to them—much to Shweta's relief.

'Let's see if we can get this bunch off the boats and into the village without anyone falling into the water.' She gave Shweta a friendly nod. 'Where's that idiot Mona? I believe she was busy gawking at the race while one of the guest boats was about to tip over.'

'It wasn't so bad,' a scarlet-face Mona muttered. 'I did let my attention wander a bit, but Nikhil stepped in.'

'Well, you're lucky he was in a good mood or you'd be hunting for a job right now,' Payal said. 'Come on— start announcing the docking order and get those snake boats out of the way now. I've had enough of them.'

Wishing she hadn't overheard the conversation, Shweta headed into the resort village. People always gossiped, and event management was on the fringes of show business, where stories were that much more outrageous—probably nothing of what the two men had said was true.

She'd just ordered a carved name-plate from one of the handicraft stores and the man had promised to have it ready in fifteen minutes. She was paying for it when Siddhant came up to her.

'That's beautiful,' he said, smiling as he saw the hand-carved letters that the man had mounted onto a wooden base. 'For your flat?'

Shweta nodded. 'My old one fell off and broke.' She watched Siddhant as he picked up the name-plate and ran his fingers over the letters. Try as she might, she couldn't summon up a smidgen of feeling for Siddhant. He was intelligent, and successful, and he'd probably make someone an excellent husband some day, but meeting Nikhil had driven the last doubts out of her head. Not that she was in any way serious about Nikhil, she hastened to tell herself. The conversation she'd overheard his team having had only underlined that she didn't stand a chance with him.

'I've hardly seen you since we got to Kerala,' Siddhant was saying. 'Let's walk around the village a bit, shall we? Unless you've seen it already? You must have reached it some time before we did.'

'Not seen much of it yet,' Shweta said.

She'd have to let him know somehow that it wasn't going to work out between them—the distinctly proprietorial air he adopted when she was around him was beginning to bother her.

CHAPTER THREE

THEY WERE SITTING down to lunch when Nikhil reappeared. Anjalika was nowhere to be seen—either she'd left, or was having lunch separately. Payal had mentioned to Shweta that her contract only included a stage performance, not mingling with the guests. Nikhil didn't come across to her, however. He spent a few minutes talking to the resort manager, and then the firm's HR head nabbed him.

Shweta found herself gazing at him hungrily. His clothes were simple—an olive-green T-shirt over faded jeans—but they fitted perfectly, emphasising the breadth of his shoulders and the lean, muscled strength of his body. At that point he turned and caught her eye—for a few seconds he held her gaze, then Shweta looked away, embarrassed to have been caught staring.

'This traditional meal business is all very well, but I wish they'd served the food on plates rather than on banana leaves,' Siddhant was saying as he tried to prevent the runny lentils from spilling over on to his lap.

'It wouldn't be very traditional then, would it?' one of the senior partners said dryly.

Remembering that the man was South Indian, Siddhant rushed into damage-control mode. 'Yes, of course. It's just that I'm not used to it. The food's delicious—we should seriously evaluate the option of getting South Indian food made in the office cafeteria at least once a week.'

One of the other partners said something in response and the conversation became general. Shweta felt pretty firmly excluded from it, however. She was sitting between Siddhant and another colleague who was all too busy trying to impress his boss. Priya and the rest of her friends were sitting across the room, and they appeared to be having a whale of a time. Siddhant himself was making absolutely no effort to bring her into the conversation with the rest of the partners—evidently he felt he had done enough by inviting her to sit with them at the hallowed top table.

Her phone pinged, and Shweta dug it out of her bag to see a message from Priya. *You look bored out of your wits*, it said, and Shweta looked across to see Priya miming falling asleep and keeling over into her banana leaf.

Shweta took a rapid decision. She wasn't very hungry, she'd finished all the food on her leaf—and the server was still two tables away. 'Siddhant, I need to go and check on something,' she said in an undertone during the next break in conversation.

Siddhant looked a little surprised. 'Right now?' he asked, and his tone implied that she was passing up on a golden chance to hang out with the who's who of the firm.

'Right now,' Shweta said firmly, and escaped to the corner where Priya was busy demolishing a heap of sweetmeats.

'What happened to your diet?' Shweta asked in mock-horror. Only the week before, Priya had embarked on an oil-free, sugar-free, practically food-free diet.

Priya shrugged happily. 'The diet's on vacation,' she said. 'This stuff is way too good to resist. Where's that hunk of a childhood friend of yours? I thought you'd finally seen the light when I saw you go off with him, but here you are back with Siddy-boy.'

'Don't call him Siddy-boy,' Shweta said, feeling annoyed with Priya. 'And I just spent the morning with Nikhil—we had a lot of stuff to catch up on. I didn't "go off" with him.'

'"Catching up"? How boring,' Priya said, making a face. 'If you aren't interested the least you could do is introduce me to him properly—he's *sooooo* hot…'

'And you're *so* not available,' Shweta said, getting even more annoyed. 'You have a steady boyfriend, remember?'

'Someone's getting jea-lous,' Priya carolled, and Shweta longed to hit her.

'Lunch over?' a familiarly sexy voice asked.

She turned to almost cannon into Nikhil. 'Yes,' she said ungraciously, wondering how much he had heard. Priya had a rather strident voice, and she hadn't bothered to keep it low.

'Sorry I had to rush off like that,' he said. 'Anjalika has this habit of creating problems halfway through an event.'

'No worries,' she said, sounding fake even to her own ears. It was a phrase she'd picked up from Siddhant, and she found herself using it whenever she didn't know how to react to something. Then natural curiosity got the better of her and she asked, 'Did she want more money?'

Nikhil looked nonplussed for a few seconds, and then he started laughing. 'I can see the team's been talking. Yes, she did. But she isn't going to get it.'

The team had been saying a lot, she thought. But, looking at Nikhil, she couldn't believe that he'd trade sexual favours for a reduction in Anjalika's fee. That was as bad as being a gigolo—worse, probably, because he didn't *need* to seduce older women for money.

'Don't look so horrified,' Nikhil said, tweaking a stray strand of hair that had escaped from the barrette she'd used to tie it back. 'This business is like that. There's a lot of last-minute haggling, and you can lose all your profits if you're not careful to tie people down with water-tight contracts before you begin.'

Forgetting the fact that pulling her hair was anything but a lover-like gesture, Shweta's relief at the business-like way he spoke was overwhelming. She'd been right all along then—his team had just been gossiping.

'Nikhil, the resort manager would like to speak to you,' Payal called out.

Nikhil made an exasperated gesture. 'I'll see you in the evening, then,' he said to Shweta.

Priya made a disappointed face once he'd left. 'Very brisk and practical, that was,' she said. 'D'you think there's something wrong with you? I was hoping you were on the verge of a mad fling with him, but you talk to him like he's your cousin or something. No chemistry at all.'

'Perhaps I'm more of a physics and geography kind of girl,' Shweta retorted. 'Grow up, Priya. Not every woman goes on heat when she sees a good-looking man.'

Siddhant had come up in time to hear the latter part of her sentence and he looked completely scandalised. Good job, too, Shweta thought spitefully as she refused his offer of a lift back to the hotel.

'I'll go in the bus with Priya,' she said. 'I'm sick of sitting around while you talk shop with the other partners.'

No chemistry. Perhaps Priya was right and she was imagining things, Shweta thought as she leaned her forehead against the cool glass of the bus window. There was that kiss, though, and the way he'd looked at her when they were watching the boat race…

'Siddy-boy didn't know what had hit him,' Priya said gleefully as she took the seat next to her. Evidently she'd forgiven Shweta for the bitchy comment about not all women being like her. 'He was so sure you'd be thrilled at being offered a seat in that stuffy old van with him and the other partners. There's hope for you yet.'

Shweta shrugged. 'I was irritated, and I said it without thinking. I'll end up apologising when I see him again.'

Priya looked disappointed. 'Don't—that'll spoil everything,' she said. 'Stay away from him a bit so that he gets the message. You're definitely off him, aren't you?'

Shweta nodded. Priya was as sharp as a needle, and there was no point trying to hide it from her. Far better that she used her rusty dissembling skills to conceal the fact that she was helplessly attracted to Nikhil.

'I don't know what you saw in him in the first place,' Priya said. 'You're smart and you're good-looking—you can do a lot better for yourself.'

'Like who?' Shweta asked dryly. 'Men aren't exactly queuing up asking for my hand in marriage. If I decided to hold a *swayamvara*, I'd probably have to pay people to come.'

Priya shrugged. In her view marriage was vastly overrated—but then, she'd spent the last six years fending off offers of marriage from several men, including her long-term boyfriend. She gave Shweta a considering look. 'You know what your problem is?' she asked.

'I don't, but I'm sure you're about to tell me,' Shweta replied.

'You treat all men like they're your buddies. So then they treat you like "one of the boys" and everything goes downhill from there. You need to build an aura—some mystique.' Priya gesticulated madly. 'Or, if all else fails, some good old-fashioned sex appeal would do the trick.'

Shweta shrugged. She'd long ago come to terms with the fact that, unlike Helen of Troy, whose beauty had launched a thousand ships, hers would only be able to float a paper boat or two. She was good-looking enough—lots of people had told her that—but men regularly bypassed her to fall for less good-looking but sexier girls. Not that it had ever bothered her much. Until meeting Nikhil again she hadn't felt the pull of strong sexual attraction. She'd just assumed it was something that people had made up to sell romantic novels and movies.

'I've booked us into the spa for a massage and a steam bath,' Priya said after a while. 'I forgot to tell you.'

Shweta shook her head. 'Take one of the other girls instead,' she said. 'I'm going for a swim.'

It was almost six when they got back to the hotel, and the pool was thankfully deserted. Everyone who'd managed to get a spa booking was headed there, and the rest were in the bar at the other end of the property. Shweta ran up to her room to change into her swimsuit, and was back at the pool in a few minutes.

The water was perfect, warm and welcoming, and she automatically felt herself relax as she got in. She did the first few laps at a brisk pace, working off the day's confusion and angst as she cleaved through the water. After a while, however, she flipped over, floating aimlessly on her back as she looked up at the sky. The sun was about to set, and the sky was a mass of lovely red-gold and purple clouds. Looking at it, she felt her troubles seep away.

A muted splash told her that someone else had joined her in the water, but she didn't turn to see who it was. Only when the sun set fully and the sky faded to a dull steel-grey did she swim to the side of the pool.

'You'll shrivel up like a prune if you stay in the water any longer,' Nikhil remarked.

A sixth sense had already told her who her silent companion was, and she didn't turn her head to look at him. 'Stalker,' she said in amiable tones. She felt in her element while she was in the pool, and more than equal to dealing with her old classmate.

He was by her side in a few swift strokes. 'What did you say?' he asked, playfully threatening her with a ducking.

'You don't even like swimming,' she said. 'You told me yesterday.'

'Depends who I'm swimming with.' The lights around the pool had come on, and his eyes skimmed over her appreciatively. 'Looking pretty good, Ms Mathur.'

She was wearing a much-used one-piece black swimsuit—but in spite of its age it clung faithfully to her slim curves. He could hardly take his eyes off her. Her wet hair hung down her back, and little drops of water were rolling down her neck and into her cleavage as she leaned against the side of the pool. Involuntarily, he raised a hand and trailed it down the side of the arm nearest him.

Shweta shivered in response, slipping back into the water before he could do more. She'd got a good look at him, and he looked pretty irresistible himself. His body lived up to if not exceeded the expectations it had aroused when he was fully clothed—all washboard abs, lean muscle and sinewy arms. He looked more like a professional athlete than a businessman. His damp hair flopped just so over his forehead, dripping into his deep-set eyes and he had just the right hint of devilry in his expression—all in all, Shweta thought, she could be forgiven for thinking him pretty irresistible.

'Well?' he asked, treading water next to her. 'Are you done practising for the Olympics? Can we get out before I catch my death of cold?'

'It's not cold at all,' Shweta said, but she swam to the side of the pool. It was difficult to hold a conversation with her ears full of water, and she didn't mean to try.

Outside the pool, Nikhil looked even more impressive, towering over her as she got out of the water. He took her hand to help her out and a jolt of electricity seemed to pass from his body to hers. Realising that she was staring up at him dumbly, Shweta made as if to step away—Nikhil, however, took her by the shoulders and pulled her against his body. Slowly, he lowered his head to hers, but just when she thought he was about to kiss her he pulled away.

'Someone's coming,' he said. 'You'd better go and change. I'll see you back here in fifteen minutes, OK?'

It took her ten minutes to shower, change into shorts and a sleeveless tee and get back to the poolside. He was waiting there for her, standing with his back to the pool. He'd changed as well, into khaki shorts and a white T-shirt. His hair was still damp, and as she came up he tossed the towel he'd been holding on to a deckchair.

'I'm leaving tonight,' he said abruptly. 'I'll see you in Mumbai soon—we have that dinner date, remember?'

Shweta felt quite absurdly disappointed. 'Are you leaving right away?'

He nodded. 'Almost. It's a long way to the airport.

I wanted to say goodbye, and I realised we haven't exchanged numbers.'

'I don't have a piece of paper,' she said. 'And my mobile's back in my room.'

'Tell me your number. I'll memorise it, and I'll call you when I'm on my way to the airport,' he said. 'I'm not carrying my mobile either.'

Shweta told him her number and he listened carefully, repeating it back to her to make sure he'd got it right.

'So…I'll call you, then,' he said, turning to climb the stairs that led to the hotel.

Shweta gazed after him in disbelief, and then ran up the stairs to overtake him. 'Just a minute,' she said. 'When you say you'll call me and we'll go out for dinner, is that like a date, or something? Because I'm a little confused—you kissed me on the boat, and you were about to kiss me just now, if someone hadn't come along. But the rest of the time you act like I'm your old buddy from school—not that I was your buddy. We used to fight all the time, except in kindergarten. Actually, that's the last time I was able to figure out what you're up to—when we were in kindergarten. You've grown more and more complicated…'

Nikhil's brow creased with concentration as he tried to keep up and failed. 'I don't know what you're talking about,' he said finally.

Shweta shook her head in exasperation. 'Forget it,' she said. 'I'm making a muddle of things as usual.'

'No—rewind a bit and let me understand this.'

His eyes were amused and caressing as he looked at her, and she felt her knees go just a little bit wobbly.

'You think I'm asking you out because I want to be your *buddy*?'

'Something like that,' she muttered—and gave an undignified little squawk as she was efficiently swept into his arms.

'A buddy?' Nikhil said. 'Hmm, that's an idea. Purely platonic, right?'

Shweta could feel her heart hammering, and pressed so close against his chest she was sure he could feel it too. When he bent his head to kiss her lips she tensed, going rigid in his arms. He kissed her very lightly, as if just tasting her lips, but when she unconsciously leaned towards him the kiss grew harder, more demanding. The sensation was exquisite, and Shweta felt positively bereft when he drew away.

She took a couple of quick breaths. 'Not purely platonic, then?' she asked, fighting to keep her voice steady.

'Not platonic,' he said, and his slow, incredibly sexy smile set her heart pounding away like a trip-hammer on steroids. 'That OK with you?'

It was more than OK, but Shweta couldn't say so without sounding impossibly over-keen. Trying to play it cool, she gave him a flippant smile. 'I can live with it,' she said—and gasped as he pulled her close for another scorching-hot kiss.

'I'll see you in Mumbai, then,' he said.

And before she could gather her senses enough to reply he was off.

Shweta watched him stride into the hotel. So much for there being no chemistry between them, she thought as a feeling of pure euphoria swept over her. Somewhere at the back of her head she knew that she shouldn't rush into a relationship blindly, but just now she wanted to enjoy the moment without bothering about the future.

CHAPTER FOUR

IT WAS MORE than two weeks after she'd returned to Mumbai that Shweta managed to meet Nikhil for dinner. He'd been out of town for a few days, and then she'd had a project to finish within some pretty crazy deadlines. After that, she'd gone down to Pune to meet her dad and her aunt. Now that she was finally back Nikhil had reserved a table at a rather swanky new restaurant at the Mahalakshmi race course for Saturday evening.

'Where are you off to?' Priya asked, lounging on her bed as Shweta made yet another attempt to get her eyeliner on straight.

'Nowhere special.' She wasn't sure why she was keeping her dinner date with Nikhil a secret, but she hadn't told Priya earlier and it would be more than a little embarrassing to tell her now. 'I'm meeting a couple of old college friends for drinks, and we might go out for dinner afterwards.'

'Can I come with you?' Priya asked. 'Rahul's out of town, and I'm so bored… Maybe one of your college friends could help cheer me up?'

'Sorry,' Shweta said, shooting Priya an amused

glance over her shoulder. 'They're not your type, and we have a lot of catching up to do. I'll tell you what— I'll lend you some of my DVDs. You can watch a nice movie.'

'You have rubbish taste in movies,' Priya said moodily, going over to the drawer where Shweta kept her DVD collection. 'It's all such grim, arty stuff—no chick flicks, and you don't even have a good action movie in this lot.' She watched Shweta as she outlined her mouth with lipliner and proceeded to colour it in with lipstick.

'You're meeting a *guy*,' she said. Shweta glared at her as she broke into a wide smile.

'Of *course*—that's why you don't want me to come along! I haven't seen you make so much effort over your face in months, and you changed in and out of three dresses before you chose this one. Who is it?'

'No one you know,' Shweta said, slamming her make-up drawer shut and squirting a last bit of perfume over herself.

'Nonsense. I know everything about you.' Priya thought for a bit. 'I know! It's that hottie from the Kerala trip. What was his name again? Naveen? Nirav? No—Nikhil. That's it—you're meeting Nikhil, aren't you?'

Despite herself, Shweta felt a warm tide of colour stain her cheeks.

Priya crowed with delight. 'I knew it! I knew something was happening. Come here and let me look at you—a special date needs some special advice.'

Shweta submitted to being examined from every

angle. Priya had a good sense of style, and it wouldn't hurt to take her opinion.

'Pretty good,' she pronounced finally. 'Except you could do with a little more colour in your cheeks. And I can't believe you didn't buy a new dress. This one's nice, but you've worn it lots of times before.'

'Nikhil's not seen it,' Shweta pointed out as she warded off Priya's attempts to put some more blusher on her cheeks. 'I don't want to look like I'm trying too hard.'

She gave herself a last look in the mirror. The midnight-blue dress was deceptively simple in cut and it showed off her curves to perfection. She wore a simple diamond pendant on a white-gold chain with matching earrings, and her shoes—as usual—were the exact shade of the dress.

'Are the shoes a bit much?' she asked anxiously.

Priya hesitated. 'A little too matching-matching, but that's OK—guys never notice such stuff.'

But Shweta was already kicking the shoes off, exchanging them for strappy silver sandals.

The intercom rang, and Priya ran to pick it up. 'Your cab's here,' she said.

Shweta had called for a taxi rather than hailing a black-and-yellow cab on the street as she usually did. It was normally a half-hour drive from where she lived to the race course, but a mixer truck had broken down in the middle of the road and the traffic was terrible. In spite of that, she got there a few minutes early. Nikhil wasn't there yet, and they had arranged to meet for a drink at the bar before they went down for dinner.

Feeling a little awkward and out of place, Shweta ordered a drink and sipped at it gingerly, surveying the room. The whole building had been redecorated recently—the bar had a high wooden ceiling with fake beams and lots of *faux*-antique wooden furniture and panelling. Shweta wrinkled her nose a little. She couldn't see why places that weren't really old tried to look that way.

'You don't look pleased,' Nikhil observed as he walked up to her.

Shweta jumped, spilling a bit of her drink. 'It's the way this place is done up,' she confided. 'They've tried to make it look like an old English pub, but it's not old and it's not English—and anyway the roof's all wrong. Pubs have low ceilings normally.'

'I'll tell the architect if I ever meet him,' Nikhil said, sounding amused. 'I'd apologise for being late—but I'm not, am I?'

'No. I have a pathological fear of being late myself,' Shweta said, 'so I end up being early for everything. I've even gone to weddings where I've reached the venue before either the bride or the groom. You're looking nice, by the way.'

That last bit had just slipped out—but he *was* looking exceptionally good. *Nice* didn't even begin to cover it. He'd had his hair cut since she'd seen him last, and the new, shorter hairstyle suited him. He was wearing a striped button-down shirt open at the collar, and black formal-looking jeans. The shirt was rolled up at the sleeves, and she could see his strong forearms, with a smattering of hair covering them. The temptation to reach out and touch was overwhelming.

'So are you,' Nikhil said, sounding more amused than ever. 'That's a lovely dress.'

'But most of the other women are wearing black,' she said. 'I'm feeling terribly out of place.'

Nikhil shrugged. 'Black is like a uniform,' he said. 'Pretty boring, if you ask me. Come on—let me get you another drink.'

Shweta hadn't even noticed that her first drink had gone. Something was not quite right. Nikhil seemed a lot more formal than he had when he'd met her last— and, while he was smiling a lot, the smile didn't reach his eyes.

'Is everything OK?' she asked.

Nikhil sighed and rubbed at his face. 'It's been a crazy week,' he said. 'Sometimes I'm tempted to throw this whole thing over and go and do something else. Maybe work in an office—it's got to be simpler.'

'More stars throwing tantrums?'

He shook his head. 'I wish. That's the easiest thing to handle. No, some of my clients are delaying payments. Big corporates. Apparently they hadn't got all the internal approvals in place before they hired me, and the bills aren't getting cleared. I've had to threaten legal action in two cases to get them to pay up. It isn't hurting me right now, because business is doing well, but unless I play hardball with these guys I'll have other clients trying to take me for a ride.'

Shweta was looking mildly shocked.

He laughed. 'Let's change the topic before your eyes

glaze over and you fall asleep on the table. How was your Pune trip?'

'Pretty good,' she said cautiously. Nikhil still looked on edge, and she would bet anything that it wasn't about a few missed payments.

'Your dad happy to see you?'

'I guess so.' Her father rarely displayed any emotion, but he'd cancelled his weekly bridge game to spend time with her, and that was saying a lot. 'He's growing old,' she said. 'He was forty when I was born, so he's pushing seventy now… I get a little worried sometimes.'

Shweta had grown up without a mother, and losing her father was one of her biggest fears. She rarely spoke about it, not acknowledging it even to herself, but the expression in Nikhil's eyes showed that he understood.

She hurried on before he could say anything. 'How's Veena Aunty doing?' she asked. She knew how fond Nikhil was of his stepmother—he was probably closer to her than to his own mother.

Nikhil's face clouded over. 'I haven't seen her for a while,' he said tightly. 'I had a bit of a bust-up with my parents. She lives with them, and I'm not keen on going there if I can help it. Amma's taken their side on the whole thing.'

'Maybe she has her reasons,' Shweta couldn't help saying. She'd always thought that Nikhil was a bit too hung up on the whole being illegitimate business. She could see why it had bothered him during his growing up years, but surely it was time to let go now?

Nikhil didn't seem to have heard her. 'I asked her to move here and stay with me,' he said. 'I have a decent flat, and I could hire someone to look after her during the day. It would be so much more dignified than letting those two take care of her. I told you, didn't I, that she's pretending to be Mom's cousin now?'

'Go to Kerala and try speaking to her,' Shweta said. 'You don't need to talk to your parents unless absolutely necessary.'

'My father's told me not to come near until I've apologised to him for what I said during our last argument,' he said. He stared broodingly into space for a few minutes.

Having run out of useful suggestions, Shweta stayed silent.

After a while Nikhil shook himself and seemed to come back to earth. He took a largish swig out of his glass and turned to Shweta. 'I'm not the best of company today, am I?' he asked, forcing a smile. 'It's just that you know the whole story—it's so much easier talking to you than to anyone else...'

Of course it was. For a few seconds Shweta felt such an acute sense of disappointment that she could hardly speak. That explained why Nikhil was seeking her out, she thought. He must have kept all this stuff about his parents bottled up for years, and it would be a relief being able to pour it out to someone who knew all about it—save him the embarrassment of having to tell whoever his current friends were that he was illegitimate.

But after the first wave of anger ebbed she was able to think about it more rationally. It was natural, his wanting to talk to her. And the kisses and dinner dates—perhaps he sensed how attracted she was to him and those were his means of keeping her hooked. Unbidden, her thoughts went back to that conversation she'd overheard between members of his team.

'I'll have another drink, I think,' she said.

Her mind was working overtime, she knew—maybe she was imagining things. Nikhil got up and went to the bar to fetch a refill, and she watched him silently.

'I resented you for a long time, you know,' he said quietly after handing her the glass. 'That's why I used to give you a hard time. You were the first person who made me realise that there was something wrong with my family.'

'Me?' Shweta's voice was incredulous. 'What did I do?'

'You asked me who my real mother was,' he said. 'I told you that both of them were my moms, but you said, "Whose tummy did you live in before you were born?" Until then I think I'd believed implicitly in the "babies are a gift from God" story. So it was a revelation in more ways than one.'

'I don't even remember,' Shweta said remorsefully. 'But I can quite imagine myself saying that. I went around once telling the whole class that Santa Claus didn't exist—some of the kids actually started crying.'

'Now, *that* I don't remember,' he said, and the smile was back in his voice. 'Maybe I got off lightly, then.'

'I thought it was very unfair,' she said after a brief pause.

Nikhil raised his eyebrows. 'What was? No Santa Claus?'

'You having two moms when I didn't have even one,' she said.

There was an awkward pause, and then Nikhil said, 'I never thought of it that way.'

The realisation that he was illegitimate had tainted most of his childhood. He'd grown up in a stolidly middle-class neighbourhood and the very fact that most of the rigidly conventional people around him had felt sorry for him had been a constant thorn in his flesh. It had never occurred to him that Shweta had envied him.

'It must have been tough for you, losing your mom when you were so young.' As soon as the words were out, he wished them unsaid. Shweta's face had closed up in an instant.

'I hardly remember her,' she said. 'And my aunt was there. She took good care of me.'

She'd always been like that when her mother was mentioned, Nikhil remembered. Something made him look down at her hands and he noticed a familiar mannerism—just like she'd used to in school she was tracing out words on her left palm with the fingers of her right hand. It was something she did when she was tense. Unconsciously he leaned a little closer, to try and make out the words, but her hands clenched into little fists, and when he looked up she was scowling at him.

'I'm sorry,' he said, his voice gentle.

'You're so *annoying*!' she burst out. 'You used to do that when we were kids—try and read what I was scribbling into my hand. I hate it! No one else—'

She broke off, realising that she sounded impossibly petulant and childish. No one else had ever noticed the habit, though she did it all the time. Not her father, or her aunt, or her boss, or Siddhant. Somehow that made her feel even more annoyed with Nikhil.

'Aren't we getting late for dinner?' she asked, sounding stiff and ungracious even to herself. 'I thought you had a reservation for nine o'clock?'

Nikhil nodded and got to his feet. 'Let's go,' he said.

She didn't even feel hungry, Shweta realised as she went down the stairs.

The ground floor of the restaurant was full now—and several people seemed to recognise Nikhil, turning to wave as he escorted her to the outdoor seating area. The women gave her curious looks, and she felt acutely conscious of her off-the-rack dress and casually done hair. Everyone else was dressed far more expensively than she was, and that somehow made her feel worse than ever. The evening was turning out to be a total disaster—the quicker she left the better it would be for both of them.

'I'm not really very hungry,' she muttered, glancing down at the menu.

Supposedly the food was Indian, but she hadn't even heard of half the dishes before. Probably they were designed to appeal to the large number of foreigners who were thronging the place. Shweta cast a quick look around. Most of the tables were occupied by glitzy types, except for one where a bunch of older people were celebrating someone's fortieth birthday. They were expensively but casually dressed, and seemed very comfortable in their own skins. The woman whose birthday it was caught Shweta's eye and gave her a wink. Instantly she started feeling better.

'I like the look of that group,' she told Nikhil. 'Especially the husband of the birthday girl. He's cute.'

'He's twice your age,' Nikhil said, following her gaze.

'But so what? He looks nice. I bet he was quite a heartbreaker when he was younger. And look at him now—he's so wrapped up in his wife, and she must be about the same age as him...'

Nikhil reached across and firmly took her glass out of her hand. 'I agree. They're very cute. But you need to stop staring,' he said. 'And they're forty—not eighty. It's perfectly normal to be wrapped up in each other even at that age. I didn't know you were such a romantic.'

'I'm not romantic at all!' Shweta gave him an indignant look. 'And I'm not drunk either. So you can give me back my glass, thank you very much.'

'I didn't say you were drunk,' Nikhil said, and gave her the glass back. 'Shall I order for you? You're holding your menu upside down.'

'It makes the same amount of sense both ways,' she said, and he laughed out loud.

After he'd finished ordering and the waiter had gone away, he reached out and took her hand across the table. 'I'm sorry,' he said. 'The evening's not gone the way it was supposed to, has it?'

'I'm not sure *how* it was supposed to go,' she said, meeting his gaze squarely across the table. 'But if it was supposed to be a date it's not been very date-like so far.'

Nikhil toyed with her hand for a few seconds without looking up. Then he lifted it and gently kissed her fingers one by one, his lips lingering against her skin. Completely taken by surprise, she watched him as if turned to stone. There was something incredibly erotic about the gesture—quite suddenly the date was living up to expectations after all.

'Why did you do that?' she asked when he finally looked up, and her voice was trembling slightly.

He took his time answering, bending to press one more kiss on her palm before he spoke. 'You looked like you could do with a kiss,' he said. 'And you're too far away for me to kiss you properly. We'll have to wait until we're out of here for that.'

She tried to be annoyed at being told that she looked as if she needed kissing, but she was so strung up at the thought of getting to kiss him properly later that she couldn't bother to be upset. The rest of her appetite seemed to have disappeared as well, but she obediently picked at her food when it arrived. After the first few mouthfuls she discovered that the taste was out of the world—and that she was hungry after all.

'I like watching you eat,' Nikhil said. 'You look like you're enjoying the meal, not counting calories.'

'I'll probably be as fat as a tub by the time I'm forty,' Shweta said.

She said no to dessert, however, and Nikhil asked for the bill. Shweta was almost jigging around in impatience while he waited for his credit card to be swiped and then signed the charge slip.

'Let's go,' he said finally, and she slipped her arm in his to walk out of the restaurant.

'I'll drop you home,' he said. 'But first...'

The path to the car park was deserted, and Nikhil pulled her into his arms and kissed her very, very thoroughly. 'I've been dreaming about this,' he said huskily. 'It drove me crazy, waiting two weeks till I could see you again.'

Shweta nodded in agreement before fisting her hands in his hair and pulling his head down for another kiss. This was one situation where his new haircut wasn't an improvement—it had been so much easier to get a grip when his hair was longer. Still, she did the best she could, and he reciprocated admirably. Both of them were a little breathless when they broke apart a few minutes later.

'I wish I could take you home with me,' he said. 'But it's too soon—I don't want to rush you.'

One part of Shweta's brain was quite sure that she didn't mind being rushed—the other part, however, grudgingly admitted that he was right.

'I'll call the car,' he said.

Shweta gave him a curious look. 'You mean you'll whistle to it and it'll come to you? Like in a Bond movie?'

Nikhil laughed. 'No, I brought my driver along because I knew I'd be drinking,' he said. 'Come here—we have time for one last kiss.'

And what a kiss it was. Shweta thought of protesting that she was in no hurry, that they could spend the rest of the night in the car park as far as she was concerned, but she had to bite the words back. Also, the kisses were getting a little too much for her self-control—another few and she'd be clawing the clothes off him. It was probably best that she go home before she completely disgraced herself. Either he wasn't quite as attracted to her as he said he was, or he had super-human self-control, she thought resentfully as they waited for the driver to bring the car around.

Once they were in the car Nikhil kept his hands off her completely. After he'd foiled her first two attempts to get closer to him Shweta sat grumpily in one corner, resisting his attempts to make polite conversation.

'Are you free next weekend?' he asked as she got out of the car.

She nodded. Definitely not as attracted as she was, she thought. Next weekend seemed like aeons away, with the week yawning like a bottomless abyss in between.

'Only I don't think I can wait that long to see you again,' he said, with a laugh in his voice as if he'd gauged exactly how frustrated she was feeling. 'OK if I pick you up after work on Tuesday?'

'Tuesday sounds good,' she said politely. 'Dinner again?'

He thought it over. 'Well, I guess we would need to eat,' he said. 'Though it wasn't exactly dinner that I had in mind…'

In her high heels she was almost as tall as he was. She stood on tiptoe and put a hand to the side of his face. Slowly she brought her lips close to his mouth and pressed them there. For a few seconds he stood frozen.

Worried that he'd move away, she moved her hands up to clasp his head and deepened the kiss, leaning into him, her body pressed provocatively against his. This time his response was far more satisfactory and he returned the kiss, his lips hot and hungry against hers, while his arms held her in a possessive embrace.

A piercing whistle from an upstairs window make them break apart and look up. Priya was leaning out of the window, waving madly.

'Stupid cow,' Shweta said crossly, once she'd got over her initial embarrassment. She made a face at Priya and gestured to her to go back inside. Priya gave her a huge grin, and mimed kissing. It took a particularly hard glare to get her to shut the window and go inside.

'I'll see you on Tuesday,' she said to Nikhil, but he gave her a quizzical look. 'Why do you and Priya share a flat? You don't seem to like each other much.'

Shweta stared at him. 'She's my best friend,' she said sharply. 'I thought you'd be able to figure that out without me having to tell you.'

She was unlocking her front door when she heard his powerful car start up and she gave a little groan. She'd been stupid, she realised, snapping at him like that. But Priya was the closest thing she had to a sister, and she'd reacted without thinking.

'You're a pestilence and a disease,' she told Priya crossly as Priya came out of her room with a big grin plastered on her face. 'A foul blot on humanity. A Nosey Parker. The worst excuse for a flatmate in all creation. The only—'

'Dry up,' Priya said firmly. 'I've saved you from a

terrible fate. Just think—what if Mrs Ahuja had looked out of the window and seen you standing on the pavement, making out in public? She'd throw both of us out of the flat before you could say *hot hunk*. Which he is, by the way. But that would have only annoyed her more.'

Sidetracked for a second by the thought of their terrifying landlady having spotted her kissing Nikhil, Shweta protested, 'She should be happy! She's always nagging me to find a "good boy" and marry him and have twenty children.'

'Reached that stage, has it?' Priya teased. 'Daydreaming about marrying Nikhil and having his children…? And without doing a single online compatibility test? What have you done with the real Shweta?'

Shweta flushed. Priya had caught her checking her compatibility with Siddhant on a matrimonial website's compatibility scorer, and she hadn't let Shweta forget it. But her words brought her back to reality with a rather sickening thump. She'd been so carried away the last few weeks, she hadn't really thought things through at all. Living in the moment was all very well, but she was in real danger of falling in love with Nikhil now.

Seeing the changing expressions on her face, Priya groaned. 'I shouldn't have opened my big mouth,' she said. 'Spit it out, now. What's bothering you?'

'I'm in this way too deep!' Shweta wailed. 'I don't know what's wrong with me. I've never made a fool of myself over a man like this before.'

'Then it's about time you did,' Priya said briskly. 'It's natural, Shweta. You're young—you need to loosen up, live life a little. I fully approve of this Nikhil person, by the way. He's super-hot, and he'll be amazing in bed. Even if he doesn't turn out to be the love of your life he'll give you a rocking time.'

'I don't want a rocking time,' Shweta muttered. 'I'm not the kind of person who rocks. I'm more into stones and pebbles.'

Priya ignored her feeble stab at humour and eyed her with misgiving. 'Don't tell me you're thinking of going back to Siddhant?' she asked. 'I hope you've told him it's off?'

'I told him the day after we got back from Kerala,' Shweta said.

It had been a difficult conversation. She'd expected Siddhant to be offended, but he'd been genuinely upset and hurt, and she'd felt dreadfully guilty. Not so guilty that she'd wanted to go back to him, obviously, but enough to stay awake a couple of nights beating herself up about it.

'He thought I hated you!' Shweta burst out suddenly. 'Nikhil, I mean. Not Siddhant. He doesn't know the first thing about me.'

'We bicker all the time,' Priya pointed out reasonably. 'You can't blame him if he thought we don't get along.'

'I did an internet search on him last week,' Shweta said. 'He hangs out at celebrity parties, and there are pictures of him with all these glamorous women... There's no reason for him to choose me over them. The novelty will wear off in no time, and then where will I be?'

'Right where you are now,' Priya said. 'But at least you'll have taken a shot at making things work with him so you don't have to wonder about it for the rest of your life.'

It was sound advice, and Shweta knew it, but when she was in her room, trying to go to sleep, the doubts all crept back. She'd never had a very high opinion of her own attractions, and the more she thought about it the more convinced she was that Nikhil would lose interest pretty soon.

She dozed off finally, but her dreams were troubled with images of Nikhil striding away from her as she ran faster and faster, trying to keep up with him.

CHAPTER FIVE

'So, WHAT DO you think, Shweta?'

Shweta looked up from her notepad in alarm. Busy daydreaming about Nikhil, she hadn't heard a word of what her boss had said to her. Across the table, Priya was nodding at her vigorously, so Shweta said, 'Um, I agree, of course.'

Deepa gave her a strange look. 'Were you listening, Shweta?' she asked. 'I asked if you had any major projects lined up for this week.'

'No, I don't,' Shweta said, wondering why Priya was still making faces at her.

'Good. Then you can fly down to Delhi and take over the audit Faisal was doing. The silly man's had an accident and broken his wrist—he won't be back to work for a week at least.'

Oh, great. 'When do I need to leave?' Shweta asked, hoping Deepa would say next week, or even Wednesday.

'Well, this afternoon would be good,' Deepa said briskly. 'Then you can meet Faisal before he goes for surgery. He's in no state to give you a proper hand-over, but at least he can tell you what to watch out for.'

'Serves you right for wool-gathering during a meeting,' Priya said when they met for lunch a couple of hours later. 'Have you told Nikhil?'

Shweta nodded glumly. 'I won't be able to see him for a few weeks now,' she said. 'He's leaving for Europe this Saturday, and he isn't back till the end of the month. *Damn* Faisal and his stupid wrist—he should have more sense than to go around breaking bones at his age.'

'It was hardly his fault,' Priya said. 'From what Deepa said, someone had spilt a drink on a dance floor and he slipped.'

'Whatever,' Shweta said, in no mood to be sympathetic. 'Pretty mess he's made of my plans.'

When she actually saw Faisal, though, she felt quite sorry for him. He was in a lot of pain, having broken his wrist in three places, and obviously terrified about going through surgery.

'Deepa must be furious,' he said, smiling up at Shweta wanly. 'This is a complicated audit, and now you've had to come down to take care of things. There'll be an additional cost which we can't bill to the client...'

'Stop stressing about it,' Shweta advised. 'Deepa knows you didn't fall down on purpose, and she'll figure out a way of recovering the costs. She's pretty smart about that sort of stuff.'

In the evening, while she was headed back from her client's office to the company's guest house, she couldn't help thinking that she could have been with

Nikhil instead. He hadn't even called—maybe he was going out with someone else instead. The thought almost made her stop in her tracks.

'There's a parcel for you,' the guest house clerk said as she came in. 'And you didn't leave your room keys with me this morning, so your room's not been cleaned. Should I send someone in now?'

'Yes, sure,' Shweta said, eyeing the parcel in puzzlement. It was a square box, done up in white paper, and it had her name on it in big bold letters. No courier slip or post office stamps. 'Who brought this?'

The clerk shrugged. 'A delivery boy. I thought it was someone from your office.'

Shweta picked up the surprisingly heavy parcel and carried it to her room. Her firm had a small office in Delhi—perhaps Deepa had asked for some files to be sent over.

But the parcel wasn't from Deepa. Opening it, Shweta was more puzzled than ever. There was a book of Urdu poetry on top—one that she'd wanted to read for a while but which wasn't available in Mumbai—and next to it was a box of expensive chocolates and a silk pashmina shawl. Under the shawl was a leather jewellery box that opened to reveal a pair of really beautiful earrings in antique silver. Right at the bottom of the box she found one of Nikhil's business cards. There was no note.

Shweta slowly put everything back in the box except for the book, which she put on her bedside table. The gifts were lovely, but Nikhil hadn't called or messaged her since she'd left Mumbai. Picking up her phone, she sat lost in thought for a few minutes. She could call *him*, of course—thanking him for the gifts would be the perfect excuse. On the other hand she might come across as being a little over-eager, perhaps even desperate. She wasn't sure of her feelings for Nikhil yet, and she'd already gone much further with him after two dates than she would have with anyone else.

In exasperation at her own indecisiveness she picked up her phone and dialled Nikhil's number before she could change her mind. It rang for a long while, and she was about to give up and put the phone down when he answered.

'Hey, Shweta,' he said. His voice was like liquid silk, making her go a little weak at the knees. Just as well she was already sitting down if two words could make her feel like this.

'Hi,' she said softly. 'Just called to thank you for the gifts—they're lovely.'

'Glad you like them,' he said. 'I told a girl in my Delhi office what to get. She's got pretty good taste.'

Shweta winced. It had crossed her mind that the gifts had been bought by someone else—there hadn't been time for him to buy the stuff himself *and* have it shipped over. She wondered what the girl had thought—the one Nikhil said had 'good taste'. Had she done this before? Bought gifts for Nikhil's girlfriends? Or had he given her some other explanation? Maybe that Shweta was a client, or an old friend? The last had the added advantage of being actually true. She couldn't help wondering how Nikhil would react if she told him that she didn't *like* the thought of one of his employees having to buy gifts for her.

'How did she find the book?' she asked instead. 'I checked with practically every bookstore in Mumbai, and I tried ordering it online as well.'

'She spoke to the publisher,' Nikhil said. 'The book's out of print, but he had some copies.'

'Well, thank her from me,' Shweta said, feeling awkward. 'The earrings are lovely too, and so is the shawl—'

'I'm missing you,' Nikhil said, cutting her off before she could mention the chocolates.

He'd had the gifts sent to her on impulse, and he was wondering whether it had been such a good idea after all. Maybe flowers would have been a better bet. But with a major product launch event starting in just under fifteen minutes he didn't have much time to speak to her.

'Nikhil, darling, I need some help.'

Nikhil turned around, cursing under his breath. The voice belonged to a singer who'd recently won an all-India reality show—she was hugely popular, and Nikhil had engaged her for several events. She was rather high-maintenance, and presumably something about the current arrangements was not to her liking.

'Give me a moment,' he said into the phone. 'What's wrong, Ayesha?'

She pouted prettily, making Nikhil grit his teeth.

'Your tech guys aren't letting my accompanists set up—they're saying that there's some dance number billed just before mine. Come on, Nikhil, I need you!'

'Right,' he said, and then, into the phone, 'Shweta...'

'You need to go.'

It was like Anjalika dragging him away in Kerala—except that this Ayesha woman sounded even more irritating.

'I don't think I'll be free till after twelve. Speak to you tomorrow, OK?'

'OK,' Shweta said. 'And thanks for...' But he'd already rung off.

When Nikhil called her the next afternoon Shweta was in a meeting and couldn't take the call. She tried calling him back once she got home. He was on his way to the airport. There were other people with him, and he sounded so distracted that Shweta finally told him she'd speak to him once he got back from Europe.

The rest of the week was intensely depressing. One of her client meetings turned acrimonious, and she had to drag Deepa and the client company's finance director into a conference call to sort things out. To say that neither of them was pleased was a serious understatement. The worst thing was that she knew no one in Delhi. She didn't feel very safe going around alone after it was dark, so she ended up staying in the guest house and watching TV every evening.

'I'll start sticking straws in my hair and talking to the walls soon,' she complained to Priya when she called. 'Even Faisal's gone back to Mumbai.'

'What news of the boyfriend?' Priya asked. 'No e-mails or phone calls?'

'None,' Shweta said glumly. 'He's in Greece. He's

probably forgotten all about me. And don't call him that. He's just an old friend.'

Priya snorted disbelievingly. 'Yeah, right—that's why the two of you had your mouths glued together the other week. Don't give up so easily.'

After Priya rang off Shweta looked at her phone thoughtfully for a while. There was nothing stopping *her* from calling or messaging Nikhil. Well, maybe not calling. She only had Nikhil's India mobile number. International roaming rates were terribly high—however rich he was now, Nikhil might not appreciate shelling out a small fortune just to hear her voice! Messaging, then.

She spent a few minutes composing a suitably witty, non-desperate message in her head. Finally she gave up, and went with, *How are things?*

Her phone rang after a few seconds and she picked it up, annoyed to find her hand shaking a little.

Nikhil's warm voice said, 'You wanted to know how things are?'

Feeling quite idiotically happy to hear his voice, she said, 'I didn't mean to disturb you. Just hadn't heard from you for a long while... Isn't it crazily expensive, calling from your India phone?'

'Ah, well, if I'd called from a local number you wouldn't have known it was me,' he said. 'And then you wouldn't have picked up the phone, and I wouldn't have got to speak to you.'

'You can call me back if you want,' she suggested.

Nikhil laughed. 'No, it's cool. Are you still in Delhi or have they let you come back home?'

'Still in Delhi. I'll be here for at least another week.'

Her voice must have sounded particularly mournful, because his softened immediately. 'Bear up—you'll hardly notice the time go by. Don't you have friends there?'

'No,' she said, and then, worried that she was turning maudlin, went on, 'But that's OK. I'm having a lot of fun exploring the city. How's Greece? Been partying a lot?'

'I've been working my backside off,' Nikhil said. 'This has to be one of the most difficult trips I've ever had to co-ordinate. And it doesn't help that I've been missing you like mad.'

Her heart suddenly thumping a lot louder than normal, Shweta said, 'I've missed you too.'

There was a longish pause.

'I'll be back in Mumbai around the same time as you,' he said softly. 'I'm looking forward to seeing you again.'

She was looking forward to it too, more than anything ever before, but she was worried her voice would betray too much emotion if she said so.

'Why's this trip turning out to be so difficult?' she asked instead, and she could hear the amusement in his voice when he answered.

'It's a huge sales convention for an insurance company. Very traditional Indian guys, half of them are vegetarian, and they want Indian food everywhere they go. I've had to fly out a platoon of cooks and enough rice and *dal* to feed the entire population of Bangladesh for the next three years. They want to dance to

Bollywood music every night till four in the morning, and the DJ's threatening to quit because he was hired for only two nights. And of course there's all the minor stuff, like equipment breaking down, or the hotel booking two men and a woman into the same room… Anyway, it's all sorted now, which is the main thing. And they've already confirmed that they'll hire us for their next convention.'

He sounded remarkably cheerful for someone who had such a lot to deal with, Shweta thought. She was getting the shudders even listening to him—she was the kind of person who couldn't bear the smallest thing not going according to plan.

'Poor you,' she said sympathetically. 'Any more star tantrums?'

'Anjalika's here,' Nikhil said. 'No tantrums yet, but we had to hike her fees up from what we paid her last time.'

An unfamiliar little dart of jealousy shot through Shweta. Anjalika and he had been featured in yet another glossy magazine article, in which Nikhil had been referred to as one of Mumbai's most sought-after bachelors and Anjalika as his 'constant companion'. Heroically suppressing the urge to say something bitchy, she said, 'I guess she's good at what she does, so it's OK.'

Nikhil wasn't fooled. 'She's just someone I work with,' he said. 'Don't let the gossip get to you.'

'I haven't heard…I mean, I have…but…' She floundered to a halt, feeling very grateful that Nikhil couldn't see her. It was bad enough reading every article about him with the eagerness of a celebrity stalker—his knowing she was doing it was a thousand times worse. 'Sorry,' she said. 'I couldn't help overhearing some of the people in your team when we were in Kerala.'

'Let me guess—they said that Anjalika works with me because I sleep with her?' She didn't answer and he said exasperatedly, 'She was the first celebrity who agreed to appear in one of my shows. She was short of cash and I paid her thrice her normal rate, but it's not something I've discussed with the team.'

'I guess it's a tough business,' Shweta said, feeling even more embarrassed by the explanation.

'Hmm...I could have always taken up a nice, normal nine-to-five job,' he said. 'Like my parents wanted me to. As my father says, I've no one to blame for where I am other than myself.'

Nikhil probably earned more than the rest of their high school class put together, but his father had still been disappointed that he hadn't taken up engineering or medicine. That was part of the reason why Nikhil hadn't spoken to his father for so long.

'I think you're doing pretty well,' she said. 'Even if your dad doesn't admit it, he must be very proud of you.'

'Oh, I doubt it,' Nikhil said lightly. 'Look, I need to go now. I have a whole bunch of insurance salesmen bouncing in and out of the Parthenon, and I need to make sure they don't do any damage.'

Shweta said goodbye to him, but she was sure he'd rung off because of what she'd said about his father. She'd met Mr Nair a few times in her schooldays, and he'd struck her as a rather nice man. Nothing like the cold-hearted villain Nikhil was making him out to be. And Nikhil's mom had been nice as well, though a little quiet and shy.

Nikhil had been right. The following week did pass by in a blur. On Thursday, though, Shweta began to get a nasty tickling feeling in her throat, and by the time she left the office on Friday she had a full-blown attack of sinusitis.

'Go home and drink lots of hot soup,' the finance director advised her during the closing meeting. 'It's the Delhi winter—you Mumbaikars aren't used to the cold.'

It wasn't all that cold, Shweta thought as she trudged to the Metro station. Winter hadn't set in yet, and the weather was still very pleasant. She'd visited the company doctor and got a prescription during lunchtime, but the medicines weren't helping. By the time she got to the guest house she was feeling really ill.

'You have a fever,' the guest house cleaning lady said, after putting a work-roughened but surprisingly gentle palm on her forehead. 'Are you sure you'll be able to take the flight tomorrow?'

'I'll decide in the morning,' Shweta said.

In the morning, though, she felt even worse, and knew there was no way she could get on a flight. She'd tried a short-distance flight once when she'd had only a mild cold, and the pain in her ears and sinuses when the flight took off had been excruciating.

'Ma'am, today is OK, but we have another booking from Sunday evening onwards,' the clerk said when she told him that she'd have to extend her stay at the guest house. 'I'm sorry, but you will have to ask the company to book you a hotel.'

Deepa was most unsympathetic when Shweta called her to explain. 'For God's sake—it's just a cold, isn't it? Can't you come back to Mumbai?' She exhaled in annoyance when Shweta told her she couldn't. 'Right, I'll ask my secretary to get you a hotel booking, then. This audit project's jinxed—first Faisal, then you. You guys are toppling over like ninepins.'

The hotel was a lot more luxurious than the guest house had been, but it was centrally air-conditioned, and even after fiddling around with the controls in her room for half an hour Shweta wasn't able to get the room any warmer. Finally she gave up and crawled into bed. She almost didn't get up to pick up her phone when it rang, but habit made her walk across the room and fetch it from her bag.

'Hi, Nikhil,' she said, but her bad throat made her voice so raspy that she knew he'd hardly be able to make out what she was saying.

'What's wrong?'

'Cold,' she said. 'Sounds worse than it is.'

'OK,' Nikhil said, sounding relieved. 'You'll be back in Mumbai tomorrow, won't you?'

'I've cancelled my flight,' Shweta said, 'and checked into a hotel because my room at the guest house isn't available. I'll come back some time next week, when I'm feeling more human.'

'Don't you know anyone there at all?' Nikhil asked.

The concern in his voice made her feel a lot better immediately.

'Should I send someone across from my Delhi office to help?'

'No,' Shweta said promptly. He'd probably send the girl who'd bought the presents for her, and Shweta didn't want strangers around. 'I'll manage—I can call the hotel guys for help if it gets too bad. Anyway, in Mumbai when I fall ill I have to look after myself. I'm used to doing it.' In actual fact she'd hardly ever fallen ill since she'd started working in Mumbai, and on the few occasions she had Priya had taken care of her.

'I don't like the thought of you being there all alone,' Nikhil said.

'Come down to Delhi and be with me, then,' Shweta said flippantly.

Nikhil disregarded that. 'Are you sure there's no one you can call? What about your father and aunt?'

'I haven't told them I'm ill!' Shweta said in alarm. 'Anita Bua's a world-champion worrier, and my dad's not much better. Don't you dare let them know.'

'I won't,' Nikhil said in mollifying tones. 'I just thought it might be nice for you to have family around.'

'It's very nice when I'm well,' Shweta said. 'It's a disaster when I'm not. I'll need to put the phone down now, Nikhil. I'm a bit groggy from the medicines, and my throat hurts if I talk too much. I'll message you the hotel number—we can talk tomorrow.'

Nikhil frowned after she'd rung off. Shweta hadn't sounded well at all, and he hated the thought of her being all alone in an unfamiliar city.

Shweta was still asleep when the phone rang shrilly in her room the next morning. She tried to ignore it for a while, but whoever was calling had the persistence of a Rottweiler, and with a final groan of protest she caved in and picked up the receiver.

'Yes?' she said, in a tell-me-one-good-reason-why-I-shouldn't-throttle-you kind of voice.

'Ms Mathur?' the girl on the phone said in a disgustingly cheerful voice. 'I have Mr Nair here, waiting for you—will you be able to come downstairs?' She broke off for a few seconds to have a muffled conversation with someone, then got back on the line. 'Oh, he says that you're ill and it would be better if he could come up to your room—is that OK?'

Half asleep, for a few seconds Shweta was thrown by the unfamiliar 'Mr Nair'. The only person she could think of with that name was her neighbour in Mumbai—he was a curmudgeonly lawyer in his mid-sixties, and she couldn't for the life of her imagine why he'd landed up at her hotel, asking for her. Then she woke up fully and realised that the girl meant Nikhil.

'I'll come downstairs,' she said, and then remembered that she looked an absolute fright. 'Actually, no—maybe you should send him up. Or—wait...not right now. Ask him to come up after ten minutes or something. I've only just got up...' She trailed off, aware that she was making a fool of herself.

The girl seemed to understand, however. 'Sure thing,' she said, and this time her cheerfulness didn't grate on Shweta's nerves.

With the prospect of meeting Nikhil in a few minutes the day seemed a lot brighter—even her throat didn't seem to hurt quite as much. She pushed the bedcovers back and went into the bathroom, washing and brushing her teeth in record time. She grimaced at her reflection. She very rarely fell ill, but when she did she made a thorough job of it. Her hair looked stringy and unwashed, and her eyes were puffed up, as if she'd been on a week-long drinking binge. Along with her hollow cheeks and chapped lips, they made her look like something the cat had dragged in.

The doorbell rang before she'd had a chance to do anything more than comb her hair and pull it back into a neat but rather limp and lifeless ponytail. Making a face at her wan reflection in the mirror, she went to open the door.

'Don't scream in fright. I've only just woken up,' she announced to Nikhil. Then she caught sight of the chocolates and flowers in his hands. 'Ooh, for me?'

'I was thinking of popping around to the Prime Minister's house with the flowers,' Nikhil said, strolling in and shutting the door behind him, 'but if you like them you can have them instead.' His face softened as he took a good look at her. 'Poor thing,' he said. 'You've lost weight since I saw you last, and your voice sounds awful.'

Shweta grimaced. 'Thanks—you're so tactful. How did you land up in Delhi?' Nikhil was still looking right at her, and there was a quality in his gaze that made her blush in confusion. 'I mean…I thought you were supposed to be in Mumbai. That's what you said when we discussed it last.'

'I was,' Nikhil said, reaching out and taking the flowers from her to put them on a table. 'But I thought

I'd come and check on you first. I've always had a thing for damsels in distress. Especially when they have deep, mannish voices and are wearing purple pyjamas.'

'Deep, *husky* voices, you mean,' Shweta said. She was having trouble keeping her voice steady. The thought of him having changed his plans to come and check on her was so moving that she took refuge in flippancy. 'And these pyjamas are the latest in chic nightwear. All the best people are wearing them—even in the day.'

Nikhil nodded seriously. 'I especially like the effect of the matching *chappals*,' he said, indicating her fluffy purple flip-flops. 'The green scrunchie is spoiling things a bit, though.' He got up and moved closer to her. 'Feeling any better?' he asked, reaching out to stroke her hair.

Quelling a mad impulse to press her lips into his palm, she nodded. 'Yes,' she said—and, before she could help herself, 'Oh, Nikhil, it's so good to see you!'

She wasn't sure who made the first move, but the next second she was in his arms, with her face pressed against his chest. He held her close, pressing his lips into her hair, moving his hands first soothingly and then rather excitingly over her back. She clung to him, inhaling the fresh clean scent of his body, nuzzling closer as he moved her into a more comfortable position. The material of his T-shirt was soft against her face, and she could feel the taut muscles of his chest through it.

'You'll catch a cold too,' she said, her much-maligned voice muffled against his chest. 'And stop kissing my hair. I haven't washed it for three days. I have just brushed my teeth though.'

Nikhil laughed at that, and gently tipped her face upwards. All thoughts of flippancy flew from her mind as she looked up at him, and she gave a little gasp when he brought his head down and kissed her very, very thoroughly. When he broke the kiss, moving his head back a little, she knotted her hands firmly in his hair and pulled his head down again. He succumbed without a protest.

'I wasn't intending to do this,' Nikhil said when they finally broke away from each other. 'You're not well. I just meant to make sure you have everything you need...'

'I have everything I need now,' she said, her eyes dancing as she reached out for him again.

He shook his head and took a firm step back. 'Be sensible,' he said.

'I'm not going to launch myself at you and rip off your clothes,' she said, a little annoyed at the way he'd stepped back. It was a pretty tempting idea, ripping his clothes off—though maybe not just now. Without his arms to support her she was feeling a bit dizzy. The virus evidently wasn't done with her yet. Unobtrusively, she started backing towards a chair to sit down. It wouldn't do to faint immediately after kissing him. It would give him entirely the wrong idea.

'Are you OK?' he asked.

So not as unobtrusive as she'd hoped after all. 'Just a little light-headed.'

'Have you eaten?'

She hadn't, and the guilty look on her face gave it away.

Nikhil gave a disgusted shake of his head. 'And here I am, grabbing at you like some sex-starved maniac. Let's get you something to eat first, and then we'll take you to a doctor.'

'It's OK—' she began to say, but her voice wasn't up to so much exercise and trailed off in an unlovely croak. Nikhil had ignored her anyway, and picked up the phone to order soup and toast from room service.

'Don't talk for a bit,' he advised once he got off the phone. 'I'll put your things together, and once you've had your soup we can get you checked out of the hotel.'

Shweta gave him an alarmed look. 'I have a small flat in Gurgaon,' Nikhil said. 'It's a bit of a drive, but I'll be able to look after you properly there.'

It sounded lovely, being looked after properly by Nikhil. He waited till she nodded, then said, 'I'll head back to Reception, then. Tell them to get the bill ready.'

Shweta watched him as he left the room. He was pretty amazing, she decided. The perfect combination of looks and charm and devil-may-care attitude.

The soup arrived, and after she had swallowed the last spoonful Shweta decided to test her voice again. 'The quick brown fox...' she started to say to the empty room, but her voice refused to rise above a whisper. Sighing, she got up to collect her scattered belongings and push them all higgledy-piggledy into her suitcase.

Nikhil came back when she was almost done with her packing. 'I thought I told you I'd do the packing for you,' he said. 'Go and get changed. I've arranged for a car.'

Shweta held out a hotel notepad to him on which she'd written, 'Have lost my voice.'

'A woman who can't answer back—perfect,' he said.

She punched him in the arm.

To her annoyance, he didn't even react, merely saying, 'D'you need help getting ready?'

She shook her head. If she'd had the use of her voice she would have asked him exactly what kind of help he was offering, but writing the question down wouldn't have nearly the same impact. Instead, she picked up jeans and a T-shirt and went into the bathroom to change.

It was a long drive from Connaught Place to Gurgaon, and Shweta dozed on Nikhil's shoulder for most of the way. It was a relief to have everything taken care of for her. Nikhil had even paid her hotel bill, refusing to look at her scribbled notes asking him how much she needed to pay him back.

'We've reached my flat,' Nikhil said gently as the cab pulled up in front of his apartment building.

Shweta woke up and groggily got out of the car. She was trying to help the driver get her suitcases out when Nikhil firmly steered her towards the lobby of the building. A teenage boy was waiting for them with Nikhil's keys.

'I've cleaned the flat and stocked the fridge with food,' the boy said. 'Take a look, and if you need anything else give me a call.'

'Thanks, Krishna,' Nikhil said. 'Shweta, take the

keys and go upstairs—the flat's on the sixth floor, to
the left of the lift. I'll pay the driver and be up in a minute with your suitcases.'

It was only when she was in the lift without Nikhil's
supporting arm under her elbow that Shweta realised
quite how ill she was feeling. Her head felt as if it was
stuffed with cotton-wool, and her knees had a distinct
wobble in them. She only just about managed to get
into the flat and collapse onto the sofa. When Nikhil
came in a few minutes later, she was already fast asleep.

Nikhil stood looking at her for a few minutes. She
looked very young and defenceless as she slept, with
her long lashes fluttering slightly with every breath and
her hair spread around her in absolute disarray. He wondered what he was doing, bringing her into his home.
He'd had more than his fair share of female company
in the years since he'd left home and struck out on his
own. Except for one short, relatively serious relationship, all his women had made it clear that they wanted a
good time and not much else. He'd told himself he liked
it better that way—love was for wimps. Now, however,
the feeling that was overcoming him was a perilous
mixture of attraction, affection, and good old-fashioned
lust—it was difficult to sort the three out in his head.

Shweta shifted in her sleep, almost rolling off the
sofa, and Nikhil was by her side in an instant. Deciding
that she'd be a lot more comfortable in bed, he picked
her up, being very careful not to wake her, and took
her into the bedroom. She nestled closer to him as he
tried to put her down on the bed, her hands curling into
the material of his shirt. Finally he lay down next to

her, gently removing her hands only once she'd settled down into a deeper sleep. Then he tenderly kissed her on the forehead and left the room.

CHAPTER SIX

'I FEEL PERFECTLY healthy now,' Shweta announced. 'And you're pampering me silly. I won't know what to do the next time I fall ill.'

'Call me,' he said, and his lips curved into an absolutely heart-stopping smile. 'No reason for you to look after yourself if I'm around.'

They were sitting across from each other at the breakfast table in his Delhi flat. It was five days since he'd come back from Greece and rescued her from the hotel, and he'd pulled out all the stops to make sure she'd got everything she needed to recuperate. She felt disloyal even thinking it, but Nikhil had been a lot more caring than her father or her aunt had ever been when she fell ill growing up. That was one of the disadvantages of being a doctor's daughter—illnesses were treated in the most matter-of-fact and unsympathetic way possible, even if her father was eaten up with worry inside.

Shweta gave him a saucy wink. 'If you promise to come over and look after me I don't mind falling ill every weekend.' Then, more seriously, she added, 'I haven't thanked you properly, have I? Other than Priya, I can't imagine any of my other friends doing so much for me.'

'They haven't known you since you were four,' Nikhil said. 'And they haven't spent their entire childhood being beaten up by you either.'

'Spent their entire childhood...' Shweta spluttered at him for a few seconds. '*You* were the one who used to drive me up the wall with your teasing and your stupid jokes. And I don't believe you've changed either.'

He laughed. 'Oh, I have,' he assured her. 'In more ways than one. By the way, I meant to tell you—you're looking pretty good this morning. Are you warm enough?'

His gaze swept over her, and Shweta felt a familiar little jolt of electricity go through her. They'd been living in the same flat for several days, but until now he'd made no move even to touch her—she could have been sixty years old for all the notice he'd taken of her. In a fit of pique she'd pulled out the shortest pair of shorts she'd brought with her and worn them today—they were a cheerful shade of pink, and she'd put on a T-shirt and a black knitted top over them. The Delhi winter was setting in, and her legs *were* beginning to feel a bit chilly, but she'd freeze to death before she admitted it.

'I'm warm enough. Thanks for asking,' she muttered. Really, he was overdoing his concern over her health—he sounded as if he was her uncle or something. It was as if the earlier Nikhil had vanished, along with the passionate kisses and the scorching looks. Now that she was feeling human again, Shweta was pretty sure she wanted the old Nikhil back.

'You don't need to thank me,' he said dryly. 'Just make sure you don't forget what the doctor said.'

The doctor had been pretty scathing about modern lifestyles and young women who let their immunity levels fall because of over-work and irregular meals.

Shweta winced. 'I'm not likely to forget,' she said. 'I was expecting him to ask for my dad's number so that he could call and tell my father what a dreadfully careless person I am.'

'He still might do that,' Nikhil said, getting up from the dining table. 'Now, are you sure you aren't cold?'

'I'm sure,' she snapped.

'What a pity,' he said. He was standing behind her now, only a few inches away, and she had to twist her body around to look up at him. 'I'd thought of some interesting ways of keeping you warm—especially since you're all recovered from your flu. But if you're sure…'

His voice had changed—became husky, caressing, and very, very sexy—but he was moving away from her. Never good at reading between the lines, Shweta found the conflicting signals frustratingly confusing.

'I *am* feeling a little chilly,' she blurted out.

He laughed, his eyes sparkling with devilry. 'So should I put the heaters on?'

For a few seconds Shweta felt positively murderous. This was like a grown-up version of the teenage Nikhil—making suggestive remarks, and then pretending he'd said nothing out of the ordinary. It was like flirting in reverse. Deciding that stamping her foot or

throwing a plate at him would be childish and imma-
ture, she sulked instead, turning her back to Nikhil
and pretending to be very busy clearing up the breakfast things.

Nikhil gave her an amused look. He knew pretty
much exactly what was going through her mind. When
he'd brought her home from the hotel she'd been so
ill that getting her back on her feet had taken priority over everything else. It had been tough having her
in the house and not even touching her, but he'd been
very careful not to take advantage of her weakened
state. Now, of course, she was fully recovered, and he
couldn't resist teasing her a little.

He came to stand right behind her as she plonked
dishes into the sink. She was muttering under her
breath, and he leaned closer and said, 'Sorry, I didn't
catch that.'

Shweta jumped a few inches into the air—Nikhil
could move very silently when he wanted, and she
hadn't heard him come up behind her. 'I wasn't talking to you,' she said.

'But I want you to talk to me.' His voice was pur-
posely mournful as he put his hands on her soapy forearms.

'I'm doing the dishes.'

'We'll ask Krishna to come and do the dishes later,'
he said, lowering his head and kissing the nape of her
neck very, very gently.

She could feel his breath ruffling her hair, and she
firmly repressed an urge to drop the dishes and turn
into his arms. 'You exploit Krishna.'

'Hmm…actually, on second thoughts, maybe I don't want him hanging around after all.'

His hands had moved from her arms to her waist. She just needed to lean back a little to be pressed up against his long, hard body…

'Maybe I'll help you do the dishes,' he was saying now. 'Then we can…umm…do other things.'

'Play Scrabble?' Shweta asked sweetly, and turned the kitchen tap on.

Oops—bad move. In her agitation she'd turned it too far, and a Niagara of water came gushing out. It splashed over the dishes, almost completely soaking the front of her black top. Nikhil leaned over her and turned the tap to a more reasonable setting. Taking her hands, he started rinsing the soap off. He did it very carefully and slowly, holding each hand under the water and running his own hands over it in a slow and sensuous movement that had her squirming against him in no time. Then, without releasing her, he reached out for a towel, and started drying her arms—still very, very, slowly. When that was done he turned her around to face him.

'You're completely…wet,' he said.

There was absolutely nothing suggestive about his tone, but Shweta shivered as he took the hem of her top and gently drew it upwards. She was wearing a T-shirt under it, and was still perfectly well covered when he got the top off and tossed it into a corner of the kitchen—she felt bare, though, when his warm gaze roamed over her body.

'Come to bed with me?' he asked softly.

For a few seconds Shweta's traditional upbringing reared its head, and she almost panicked and said no—but this was Nikhil. She'd known him all her life. She trusted him. Looking into his warm brown eyes, for the first time she began to think that she was probably in love with him, and with that realisation her last doubts fell away.

'Yes,' she said, and she sounded confident and very sure of what she wanted.

In the next second she was in Nikhil's arms. He held her very close for a few seconds, and then he swung her up into his arms and carried her to the nearest bedroom.

'I'm hungry,' Shweta announced, propping herself onto one arm and lazily trailing a finger down Nikhil's hair-roughened chest.

It was the middle of the afternoon, and the last few hours had been the best hours of her life. Far more experienced than her, Nikhil had been very gentle at first, careful not to alarm her. But, finding her eager and willing, he'd finally abandoned all restraint. Shweta's lips curved into a smile as she remembered quite how good it had been.

'Hungry, are you?' Nikhil frowned at her. 'Are you likely to turn cannibal? Should I be worried?'

Shweta laughed, and leaned down to nip at his lower lip lovingly. 'Mmm, that's a thought,' she said. 'You taste pretty good, actually...'

'I'll get up and cook lunch for you,' Nikhil said, sitting up in mock-haste and taking her with him. 'Just think—you might want to do this again some day, and if you eat me up you'll have to find a new man. He might not be quite as nice as me.'

Shweta pretended to think.

'I cook quite well,' Nikhil said as added inducement. 'And I'm house-trained—you won't regret it.'

'Can you do rice and noodles? With mushrooms?'

'Yes, ma'am, of course I can.' Nikhil paused to drop a row of little kisses on her shoulder, but raised his head as she spoke. 'And you can have chilli chicken with it, if you like. And ice cream. But I didn't make that—it's already in the freezer.'

'The ice cream is the clincher,' Shweta said. 'I'll allow you to live.'

Nikhil gave a mock sigh of relief and tried to get out of bed—Shweta pulled him back for a kiss.

'I thought you were hungry,' he protested as he found himself back in bed, with Shweta draped seductively over him.

'I can wait for a little bit,' she said. 'Right now you've got me interested in *you* all over again.'

It was late afternoon by the time they finally made it to the kitchen, and by then both of them were too hungry to bother about cooking an elaborate meal.

'Scrambled eggs. Or omelettes and bread,' Shweta decided after doing a quick scan of the fridge. She gave him a doubtful look. 'Did you mean it when you said you can cook? Because I'm not all that good. Priya does most of the cooking at home.'

'I meant it,' Nikhil said. 'I'm not *cordon bleu* level, exactly, but I can manage.'

He could do more than manage, Shweta decided as

she bit into a delicately flavoured omelette. There was a lot more to Nikhil than met the eye. 'Any other talents I should know about?' she enquired. 'Singing, maybe? Ballroom dancing?'

'Someone did try to teach me to jive once,' Nikhil said. 'Mrs Fernandes—remember?'

She did. Shweta had been his partner in a dance their class had been rehearsing for the school annual day. Mrs Fernandes had paired them up because, in her words, 'that boy' behaved a little better with Shweta than he did with the other girls. Shweta had been deeply annoyed, but Mrs Fernandes had known her father and she hadn't dared to protest. And because Mrs Fernandes had been well over fifty at the time, jiving had been the only 'Western' dance style she knew well enough to teach the class.

'I got expelled before that annual day, didn't I?' Nikhil asked. 'Who did you end up dancing with? Vineet?'

'I didn't participate,' Shweta said. 'Dancing wasn't really my thing.' She had been pretty upset when Nikhil was expelled—especially when she'd found out that her father had been on the disciplinary committee. She hadn't ever said anything to her father, but that was the first time that she'd seen him as a regular human being, capable of making mistakes.

'They weren't fair to you, expelling you like that,' she said.

Nikhil gave her a lazy smile. 'Oh, I think they were. I'd pushed their patience to the brink.'

'Vineet and Wilson were with you when you stole that bike,' she said.

She waved him aside impatiently when he murmured, 'Borrowed...'

'And Wilson used to smoke as well—all the time.'

'They were a lot smarter than I was,' Nikhil said, getting to his feet. 'And they didn't go looking for trouble.' He surveyed her mutinous expression. 'I don't hold it against your dad, if that's what you're worried about,' he said.

Shweta gave an impatient shrug. 'He's so...so...*set* in his ways,' she said. 'It doesn't even occur to him that he could be wrong about anything.'

Nikhil leaned across to take her plate. 'Finished?' he asked, and when she nodded her head, he said, 'Still like that, is he?'

Shweta nodded. 'It's my fault as well. I shouldn't bother so much about what he thinks. I don't even live at home now, and to be fair to him he's stopped trying to tell me what to do. But he has an opinion on everything, from my job to my clothes. He even had something to say when I chucked away those dreadful glasses and started wearing contacts.'

'How about your boyfriends?'

Shweta gave him an enquiring look.

'Does he have opinions about your boyfriends as well?'

'I'm sure he would, if I introduced any of them to him,' Shweta said.

Nikhil noticed that she was doing the scribbling

thing again—tracing words out on the palm of one hand with the fingers of the other.

'So far I've never bothered—I've not had much luck with men. I think he'd have liked Siddhant, only *that* particular story didn't go anywhere, did it?'

Nikhil nodded. If he'd been in a psychoanalysing mood there would have been a lot he could read into what Shweta was saying, but right now he had a more pressing concern.

'I assume he would be horrified if he got to know about me?' he said lightly.

Shweta shrugged. 'Not planning to tell him,' she said.

She looked a little tense, but her tone was so matter-of-fact that it took Nikhil a few seconds to absorb what she was saying. When he did get it, he felt a quick stab of anger go through him.

'Not planning to tell him now, or not planning to tell him ever?' he asked, keeping his voice carefully even.

Shweta bit her lip. She wasn't sure why Nikhil was cross-examining her—maybe he was trying to figure out how seriously she'd taken their sleeping together. And maybe he'd run for his life if he figured that she was planning to tell her family about him.

'I don't know,' she said. 'I mean, there isn't much to tell, is there? We're friends and...'

'Friends?'

'Well... Lovers, I guess. Only I'm not likely to talk to my dad about my sex-life, am I?' She might have told her mother if she'd been alive, but she didn't say that out loud.

Nikhil laughed, but there was very little genuine mirth in the sound. 'So that's all I am, is it? Part of your sex-life?'

Shweta looked at him uncertainly. She didn't recognise him in this mood, and she wasn't sure what was bothering him—he couldn't actually *want* her to tell her father that she was sleeping with him. That made about as much sense as sticking one's head into a beehive full of angry bees. Her father might have become a little less control-freaky as he grew older, but he was still rigidly conventional—he'd probably come after Nikhil with a hypodermic full of strychnine if he thought his precious daughter was being messed around with.

The thought that Nikhil might be feeling insecure crossed her mind, but she dismissed it. There was no reason for him to be insecure. She'd dropped into his arms like a plum ripe for picking. If anything, she should be the one getting clingy and emotional.

'I haven't *had* a sex-life before now,' she pointed out. 'So, if we're getting all technical about it, I'm just part of yours, aren't I?'

He didn't say anything, but his expression lightened a little. She sprang to her feet. 'Don't let's fight,' she coaxed, going over to him and putting a hand on his crossed forearms. 'I'm sorry if I said something I shouldn't have.'

Nikhil looked into her upturned face and his expression relaxed as he bent down to drop a kiss on her parted lips. 'It wasn't anything you said,' he assured her. 'Put it down to me being a little cranky.'

Shweta frowned. 'Must be the food,' she said. 'It

can't be the sex making you cranky. Or does it usually take you that way?'

Nikhil laughed and swept her into his arms. 'It most definitely doesn't.' His voice softened as he gazed into her eyes. 'You're pretty special, Shweta Mathur, do you know that?'

CHAPTER SEVEN

'WHY DON'T YOU move in with me?' Nikhil asked.

They were back in Mumbai and had been spend-ing practically every free minute together for the last three weeks. Nikhil had never been happier. There was something about Shweta that centred him—it was as if she brought peace to his restless soul. He had been toy-ing with the idea of asking her to marry him ever since they'd first kissed, and he'd made up his mind a few days back. An engagement first—perhaps a long one, to allow both of them enough time to get used to the idea of spending the rest of their lives together. Asking her to move in with him was the first step.

'Live with you?' Shweta wrinkled up her nose. 'Isn't that a little unconventional? We're in Mumbai, not Man-hattan.'

In the last few weeks she'd figured that Nikhil was a lot more serious about her than his sometimes casual attitude suggested. On the other hand, there was his rather colourful past, and her own pathological aver-sion to taking risks—taking things slowly seemed to be the only sensible thing to do.

'I know we're in Mumbai.' Nikhil pretended to be offended. 'I might not have topped the class in geography, but the little fact that I live in Mumbai hadn't escaped me... Ouch—don't. You've grown into a terribly violent little thing, Shweta.'

Shweta gave him a last punch in the arm for good measure. 'Some men deserve to be treated violently,' she said, though she reached up and dropped a light kiss on his forehead, right where her unerring aim with the blackboard duster had left a scar many years ago. 'You'd get terribly out of hand if I didn't keep a strict watch on you.'

'Yeah right,' Nikhil said. 'So, how about it? It's not all that uncommon in Mumbai nowadays—lots of people live together.'

'I must say that's the most romantic proposal I've ever received,' Shweta said. 'Actually, "So, how about it?" is probably the most romantic proposal *anyone's* ever received. It should go down in the *Guinness Book of World Records* as an example for generations to come....'

Nikhil grinned at her. 'You'd have run a mile if I'd gone down on one knee,' he said. 'But I've got you a ring.'

In the short time they'd been together he'd figured that, while she was a romantic at heart, Shweta was deeply uncomfortable with romantic gestures—somehow she didn't seem to think she was worth them. And proposing to her was important. He wanted to make sure he did in a way that made it impossible for her to refuse just because she was embarrassed.

'Let's see the ring,' Shweta demanded, but inside her heart was pounding away at triple speed. A ring meant an engagement, and she'd never allowed herself to hope that Nikhil would go that far. He'd had dozens of girl-friends, after all—some of them well-known models and actresses. There was no reason to imagine that he was serious about her.

Nikhil took the ring out of his pocket and showed it to her. It was a square-cut champagne diamond, flanked with smaller stones in a pale-gold setting. She'd told him once that she didn't like traditional solitaires, and he'd gone out of his way to find something that was unusual yet classic in design.

Shweta looked at it for a few seconds. Misunder-standing her silence, he said, 'If you don't like it I can exchange it for something else.'

'No, it's lovely,' she said, and then she looked up at him and asked. 'Are you sure about this, Nikhil?'

'I'm sure,' he said. Then, more gently, he added, 'But I understand if you need some time to think things over. There's no hurry.'

He didn't seem too fussed about the whole thing, and Shweta felt her hackles rise. There was a little pause. 'Why do you want to get engaged?' Shweta asked fi-nally.

Nikhil looked surprised. 'Why do I…? Because I care about you! Why else?'

Why else indeed. It struck Shweta that Nikhil was taking a lot for granted. She couldn't blame him—she wore her heart on her sleeve, and it was probably very evident that she was in love with him. On the other hand, she didn't know how *he* really felt.

She bit her lip. 'I care too,' she said. 'It's just that I'm not comfortable with the thought of moving in with you. I know it's hypocritical, when we're sleeping together, but I'm a little conservative that way.'

Nikhil nodded. 'Are you OK with an engagement, though?' he asked, and his lips thinned as the pause lengthened.

'Maybe not just yet,' she said. She wasn't sure herself what was holding her back—a few minutes ago she'd been thrilled at the thought of being engaged to Nikhil. But dimly she felt that if she said yes now both of them would be entering into an engagement for the wrong reasons. One part of her said that she was making a stupid mistake, while the other part desperately wanted to get away and think.

'Right…' Nikhil said.

His voice was controlled, rather lifeless, and Shweta had a sudden twinge of doubt. Maybe he wasn't as blasé about the whole thing as he seemed. She watched him as he closed the ring box and put it on the table, but his face was impassive.

'I'm sorry, Nikhil,' she said helplessly.

'Is there something in particular that's bothering you, or…?'

Shweta shook her head. 'I just feel that we should take some time and think this through properly. I'm crazy about you, but it's been only three weeks, and you know what I'm like.'

Her face was appealing as she looked up at him, and

some of the rigidity left his face. 'Little Miss Take-No-Risks,' he said, with only the faintest trace of mockery as he took her hand and kissed it gently. 'I understand. But don't keep me waiting too long, OK?'

With a little sob, Shweta threw herself into his arms. She did love him—more than she could say—and it took all her will-power not to cave in and agree to an immediate engagement.

Nikhil hesitated for a second, and then he put his arms around her and held her close. Shweta's rejection had hurt, and it was a measure of the depth of feeling he had for her that he wasn't resentful. Maybe he'd gone about it the wrong way, he thought. A romantic gesture might have worked better. But he hadn't wanted to dazzle Shweta into agreeing to marry him only to regret it later.

'I can't understand you,' Priya said in despair when Shweta told her. 'Any fool can see you're completely besotted by him. Why would you say no?'

'It's too soon,' Shweta muttered.

'And you're scared?'

Her eyes flew up to meet Priya's. 'Not scared, exactly,' she said, and then, 'Or maybe, yes—I *am* a little scared. I'm not sure what Nikhil sees in me, and I need to know it'll last. He's dated all kinds of women, and he's never stuck with any of them for more than a few months.'

'I bet he's not asked any of them to marry him either,' Priya said. 'He's a very attractive man. You can't blame him if he's played the field a little. You need to trust him.'

'What are you? His PR agent?' Shweta asked crossly. 'I just need some time to think, OK?'

Priya shrugged. 'Nothing wrong with taking time, but don't keep him hanging around for too long. He doesn't look the patient type.' Her voice gentled as she saw Shweta's stricken expression. 'I don't mean he'll dump you if you don't agree to getting engaged,' she said. 'But he won't know why you're holding back, and he might get impatient and angry. Why don't you just speak to him a little more openly? Tell him what's bothering you.'

'But I don't know properly myself!'

'Would you get annoyed with me if I told you?'

'Probably,' Shweta muttered. 'I hate it when you go into your psychoanalyst mode.'

Priya laughed. 'I'm not trying to psychoanalyse you,' she promised. 'But it's pretty obvious—your dad closed himself off from everyone when your mom died, and somehow he's made you think it's safer to have a blood-less marriage of convenience rather than expose your-self to that kind of hurt.'

Shweta felt a lump come into her throat. 'They were very happy together,' she said. 'My mom and dad. I don't remember her much, but you can tell from the photos and when he talks about her... But that's got nothing to do with me and Nikhil.'

Priya sighed and left it at that. Perhaps it was best for Shweta to figure things out for herself. At least she'd progressed enough to realise that she belonged with

Nikhil and not with someone like Siddhant—hopefully, in time, she'd learn to trust him with her heart.

Things were a little awkward between Shweta and Nikhil for the next couple of days, but soon they swung back into an easy rhythm of spending weekends together, as well as a few evenings in the week when he wasn't working.

'Amma's decided to pay me a visit,' Nikhil said one evening over dinner.

His tone was neutral, but Shweta looked up sharply. 'Just her? Or your parents too?'

'Just her,' he said. 'Though I'm sure my parents have something to do with it. This is the first time she's travelled alone—and she's just recovered from a long bout of illness. But she's insisting I don't need to go and fetch her.'

Shweta didn't think that Veena's deciding to travel alone indicated anything, but she wisely refrained from arguing the point. Nikhil tended to get completely irrational when it came to his parents.

'So, do I get to see her?'

'Yes, of course. She'll be ecstatic about seeing you again. You're probably the only person she knows in Mumbai apart from me.'

'Ecstatic' was probably an exaggeration, but Veena was definitely very pleased to meet Shweta when she arrived in Mumbai. 'It's so nice to see you!' she said, beaming all over her thin, rather careworn face. 'It's been years since I saw you last—you were just a little girl! I remember when you came home after school one day; you were so polite and respectful. Ranjini and I couldn't stop talking about you!'

Shweta smiled back at her. 'It's good to see you too, Aunty,' she said. 'Will you be in Mumbai for a while?'

Veena's face clouded. 'I'm not sure,' she said. 'Nikhil's father's not very well, and Ranjini might find it difficult to manage on her own.'

It was the second time Veena had mentioned her husband's mistress, and Shweta found that her childhood memory was perfectly accurate in this instance—there was no trace of resentment in Veena's voice when she spoke about Ranjini. Not for the first time Shweta found herself thinking that there was a lot more to the elder Mr Nair's domestic arrangements than met the eye.

'Is it serious? Nikhil's dad's illness?'

Veena shook her head. 'Oh, no. His blood pressure's a bit high, and he's due for a cataract operation in his left eye.'

'They can manage a cataract operation perfectly well on their own,' Nikhil said as he came into the room carrying three cups of coffee on a tray. 'Now that you're here I'm not letting you go in a hurry.'

Veena's eyes were frankly adoring as she looked up at Nikhil. 'Oh, thank you,' she said, taking a cup from the tray. 'You shouldn't have. I was about to get up and make the coffee.'

'I'm buttering you up,' Nikhil said, giving her a lopsided smile. 'So that you stay here for as long as possible.'

'I can stay for a couple of weeks,' Veena said. 'After

that I'm pretty sure the two of you will be tired of having me around.'

'Of course we won't,' Shweta said impulsively. 'Nikhil's been looking forward to seeing you, and so have I. It'll be fun showing you around.'

Veena smiled, but said nothing, and Shweta couldn't help feeling that she'd leave once the two weeks were over.

Nikhil was looking a little tense again, and she hurried to change the topic. 'Do you still watch Bollywood films?' she asked Veena. It had been a bit of a joke around school—Mr Nair solemnly escorting his wife *and* his mistress to the movies every Saturday.

'Ooh, yes,' Veena said, sounding more like a sixteen-year-old than a grey-haired lady in her sixties. 'Some of these new actors are quite good. But I don't like the actresses much—all they seem to do is wear tiny clothes and dance around in front of the men.'

Shweta cast an involuntary look at her own rather short skirt. She'd come over directly after office, and it hadn't occurred to her to change.

'Oh, much tinier than that,' Veena assured her earnestly, catching the look. 'You look very nice, dear. I didn't mean to make you uncomfortable.'

Nikhil caught Shweta's eye and burst out laughing. 'Oh, God, Amma, you're priceless,' he said finally. 'Poor Shweta—now she'll lie awake all night wondering if you think her clothes are tiny.'

Veena gave him a reproving look. 'No, she won't,' she said. 'Do you watch movies now, dear? I remember your father didn't let you when you were a child.'

'He lets me watch them now,' Shweta said, beginning to feel a little cross. Childhood reminiscences were OK up to a point, but she didn't like to be reminded of how hemmed-in her life had been.

'Yes, of course,' Veena said. 'I didn't mean it that way. I suppose he thought Bollywood movies weren't suitable for a young girl, and he was quite right. But when your mother was alive they used to go to the movies every weekend—just like Nikhil's father and me.'

She hadn't known that, Shweta thought, feeling a pang go through her. All her life she'd thought her father hated movies, but maybe he'd just avoided them because they reminded him of his wife.

'Your mother was so lovely,' Veena was saying. 'Smita Patil was one of my favourite actresses, and I thought your mom looked a lot like her.'

'Shweta looks a bit like her too,' Nikhil said. 'Especially the eyes.' He'd seen that Shweta was looking a little overwrought, and he wanted to steer the conversation into safer channels.

Veena gave Shweta an affectionate look. 'Yes, she's as beautiful as her mother.'

'Thanks,' Shweta said, trying to smile.

There were very few people who still talked about her mom—her father had changed houses soon after her mother died, and he'd fallen out of touch with their old neighbours and friends. He spoke about her only rarely, and his sister hadn't known her very well. Veena hadn't known her well either, but to Shweta the few sentences she'd spoken had made memories of her mother come to life. So far she'd always thought of her mother in the abstract—not as a living, breathing woman who'd gone to the movies and looked like a famous actress. Smita Patil had died young as well, and that made the comparison even more poignant.

'You OK?' Nikhil asked when Veena left the room for a few minutes to fetch something.

She nodded. 'I didn't realise Veena Aunty knew my mother,' she said softly. 'But it felt good, hearing about her.'

Shweta refused to stay to dinner, pleading an early start the next morning as an excuse.

'But I'll drop in again soon,' she promised a visibly disappointed Veena as she left. 'I still remember the prawn curry you gave me when I came over to your house in Pune.'

Nikhil came to the door to see her off, and when he pulled her close she sought his lips hungrily with her own.

'Is Priya in town?' Nikhil asked in an undertone when he released her after a few minutes. Veena's visit meant that Shweta couldn't stay the night in Nikhil's flat, and the thought of the enforced separation was sheer torture.

'Very much so,' Shweta said. 'But you can come over anyway. I have my own room, and Priya has a boyfriend of her own. She isn't around much herself.'

Nikhil hesitated. 'I thought you weren't very keen on people knowing about us,' he said.

Shweta's eyes opened wide. 'Why would you think that?' she asked. 'Anyway, Priya knows—how d'you think I explain being away for so many nights? Prayer meetings?'

He smiled briefly, but still looked unconvinced. 'We'll figure something out,' he said. 'Maybe a hotel. I don't want to put you in an awkward situation.'

'It would be far more awkward sneaking into a hotel for a dirty weekend,' Shweta said, standing on tiptoe and firmly pressing her lips to his. 'Love you, Nikhil. Bye!'

'Bye,' he said, but he stayed at the door long after Shweta had disappeared into the lift—so long that Veena came out to look for him.

'What are you doing out here all alone?' she asked. 'Is everything OK?'

Nikhil nodded, forcing a smile to his lips. 'Everything is fine,' he said. 'I'm sorry—I started thinking of something.'

Veena gave him a worried look but refrained from asking any questions. She'd looked after Nikhil since he was a tiny baby—Ranjini had been young and nervous when he was born, and more than happy to relinquish him into an older woman's care. In some ways she felt more like his real mother than Ranjini, but she was always careful not to let it show.

'What do you want for dinner?' she asked. 'I can do rice and *avial*—or *dosas*. I have everything ready.'

'Come and sit down with me for bit, Amma,' Nikhil said. 'We haven't had a chance to talk properly since you arrived—I was rushing around trying to finish work, and then Shweta came over.'

'She's a lovely girl,' Veena said warmly. 'Are the two

of you…?' She left the question hanging delicately—
she was of a generation and upbringing that didn't ask
direct questions about people's love lives.

'I want to marry her,' Nikhil said heavily. 'She hasn't
said yes yet.'

'You've asked her?' Veena had no illusions about
her husband's son, and she was a little surprised at his
saying he wanted to marry Shweta. So far he had flit-
ted from one relationship to another, and Veena had got
the impression that he was shying away from commit-
ment—she had been all prepared with a little lecture
on how he couldn't treat Shweta the way he did all his
other girlfriends.

'Of course I've asked! Amma, we've been—' He
broke off, not wanting to shock his stepmother, and
continued in bitter tones. 'I know what you've been
thinking—I could see it on your face when you were
talking to her. You were feeling all protective, and you
assumed I was playing the fool with her.'

'No, I didn't. I know you wouldn't deliberately hurt
someone, but I *was* a little worried. She seems to be…'
Veena hesitated a little '…very fond of you, and I wasn't
sure if you felt the same way.'

'I've known Shweta since she was four years old,'
Nikhil said. 'If I wasn't serious about her I wouldn't
have come within touching distance of her, let alone—'
He broke off again, because Veena was looking uncomfortable. 'Anyway, it doesn't matter. She's the one who
needs more time to make up her mind.'

'If you're already…' Veena tried to phrase it as
delicately as she could, and then, failing, hurried on.

'She's a girl. I would have thought she'd be in a hurry to marry.'

'It doesn't work that way nowadays,' Nikhil said with a short laugh. 'And I can quite see her point—her family's not terribly well-off, but they're very proud. Dr Mathur's only daughter marrying the illegitimate son of a building contractor would be a big come-down. Oh, and I got expelled as well—from a school where he was on the board of directors. Yes, I can see it going down a treat…his daughter wanting to marry me.'

Veena had turned very white. 'Is that what she told you?'

Nikhil shook his head. 'She doesn't need to say it. I know her father, and though she won't admit it I know she's completely under his thumb. She cares for me, but she's not sure if she cares enough to cut herself off from her family.' He noticed Veena's still expression and reached out impulsively, taking her hand.

'I'm sorry I started talking about it,' he said. 'It's not your fault, and I'm sure I'll win Shweta around in time.'

'Perhaps if I talk to her—' Veena started to say.

Nikhil cut her off. 'No, don't. It'll only make things worse. Now, come on, let's figure out dinner—I'll help you put something together.'

Veena allowed Nikhil to coax her into the kitchen, but she was deeply troubled. The rift between Nikhil and his parents was bad enough. The thought that Nikhil was suffering even today because of his illegitimacy was unbearable. She'd been happy when he'd set up his event management company, especially because she'd thought his background wouldn't matter in the rather bohemian crowd he mingled with. She didn't really approve of his girlfriends, with their artificially straightened hair and short dresses, but she'd hoped he would settle down with one of them. His marrying Shweta would be a dream come true. She was quite sure Shweta would come round in the end—it had been difficult to miss the depth of feeling in the girl's eyes when she looked at Nikhil. But Nikhil was the kind of man who brooded and let old resentments fester. Shweta's reluctance boded ill for a happy life together. He'd allow distrust to eat away at him—always assume she was ashamed of being seen with him.

'Stop looking so worried,' Nikhil teased, putting his arms around his stepmother and giving her a quick hug. 'What's eating you?'

'I'm trying to decide between *dosas* and rice,' Veena said. 'It's a difficult call to make—needs a lot of thought.'

'*Dosas,*' Nikhil decided. 'I've missed the way you make them.'

Shweta sighed as she put the phone down after a particularly difficult call with a client. The week had been dispiriting, to say the least. Nikhil had been busy with work, and when he hadn't, he'd had Veena to take care of. She'd tagged along a couple of times, but Veena's idea of suitable entertainment was to visit every major temple in the city, and Shweta had finally given up and gone home in sheer exhaustion. It didn't help that Veena kept giving her anxious looks. She seemed on the verge of asking her something, and Shweta was sure it had to do with her not being engaged to Nikhil yet.

That was another thing she was puzzling over. Nikhil wasn't pressuring her at all, and he'd been the perfect boyfriend so far. Yet still she held back from saying yes to him. Mainly it was because she was convinced he wasn't really in love with her. The physical attraction between the two of them was too strong to be denied, and at times it blinded both of them to anything else. Outside of it, Nikhil's eagerness to marry her could be explained by his feeling comfortable with her, just because she'd known him for so long and understood the complicated situation with his family. She suspected that he never talked about his parents with anyone else he knew in Mumbai. In spite of the wide circle of friends and acquaintances he partied with, he was essentially reserved and very lonely.

'Bad day?'

Siddhant had stopped by her desk and was smiling at her. Shweta nodded ruefully. 'The company I audited is disputing every comment on the report,' she said. 'Deepa's going to kill me when she finds out.'

Siddhant shook his head. 'Deepa's a tough boss, but she's a very fair person,' he said. 'She'll take your side.'

'I hope so.' Shweta still felt rather guilty about the way she'd treated Siddhant, especially since he'd been so nice about it. Perhaps the fact that she and Nikhil had been childhood friends helped—Siddhant hadn't reproached her even once, though he'd been shattered by the news. In the last couple of weeks they'd progressed to a polite friendship, and Shweta found herself liking him a lot more than she had when she'd been gearing herself up to marry him.

'How's Nikhil doing?'

Shweta sighed. 'Busy. Most of his big events are on Fridays or over weekends, and he needs to be around to make sure everything's running smoothly.'

'So you're not meeting up with him after work today?'

Shweta shook her head.

'Then let me take you out for dinner,' Siddhant said. 'We haven't caught up for a while, and there's no reason why we shouldn't stay friends even though…well…'

'Yes, sure,' Shweta said hastily before he could elaborate further. She had nothing else to do, and having dinner with Siddhant would help lessen the guilt she felt every time she saw him.

'Ask Priya if she'd like to join us,' Siddhant said.

He'd probably said that just to make it clear that he wasn't trying to woo her back—in any case, Priya was horrified at the thought of dinner with her and Siddhant.

'No way,' she said. 'It'll be the most awkward meal of the century, what with you having just jilted Siddy-boy. Have you told Nikhil you're going out with him?'

'No, I haven't,' Shweta said, justifiably annoyed. 'I didn't jilt Siddhant, by the way. He never even told me he was interested. And Nikhil's not the possessive kind—he won't care.'

As it turned out, though, he *did* care—he cared a lot more than Shweta had ever imagined. She'd put her phone on silent during dinner, because she didn't want

Siddhant to think she was being rude answering calls while she was with him, and the dinner had been pleasant, with both of them carefully sticking to neutral topics of discussion. Shweta couldn't help comparing him with Nikhil—Nikhil was terribly opinionated, often unpredictable, and she'd never been out for dinner with him without losing her temper at least once. But he made her feel alive and desired and cherished all at the same time. In stark contrast, her conversation with Siddhant was a mass of clichés and views picked up from the latest business magazines. Nice as he was, Shweta couldn't help thinking that she'd had a lucky escape.

It was only after Siddhant had dropped her home that Shweta checked her phone and found three missed calls from Nikhil.

'Where have you been?' he demanded when she called him back. 'I tried a dozen times. I was beginning to get worried!'

'You called me exactly three times,' Shweta said calmly. 'My phone was on silent—I'd gone out for dinner with Siddhant.'

There was a long pause. For a second Shweta thought that the call had got disconnected.

'With Siddhant?' Nikhil repeated slowly, a dangerous note coming into his voice. 'You went out for dinner with him? Alone?'

'Quite alone.' Shweta was annoyed now, and she let it show. 'Now, if you've finished cross-examining me, I'd like to go to bed. It's quite late.'

'I was planning to ditch one of my biggest launches of the year because I wanted to come and spend some time with you,' he said. 'Obviously I shouldn't have bothered. You were too busy to even take my calls, going out for dinner with your very eligible little toy-boy...'

He was almost spitting the words out—Shweta could feel the anger coming off him in waves. She could feel a reciprocal fury stirring in herself.

'I suppose I should have been sitting at home next to the phone on the off-chance you'd call?' she said. 'Grow up, Nikhil. This isn't the nineteenth century.' Irrelevantly, she wondered if they'd had phones in the nineteenth century. Perhaps not, but Nikhil was too worked up to pick holes in her logic.

'I don't expect you to hang around waiting for my calls,' he said through his teeth. 'I do, however, expect you to refrain from two-timing me with the man you were all set to marry two months ago.'

'Right—that's enough,' Shweta said, her voice absolutely cold with rage. 'I'm ringing off now, and don't you dare try to call me back. I don't think I want to talk to you ever again.'

She cut the call. Immediately the phone began to ring again, and she switched it off, her hands trembling with anger as she punched the buttons. The landline began to ring next, and she took it off the hook as soon as it stopped. Then she locked her bedroom door, so that Priya couldn't come in for a midnight chat, and plonked herself on her bed, staring into space. She was usually the kind of person who lost her temper and calmed down within a few minutes—now she was so furious she could hardly think straight.

Around fifteen minutes later she heard Priya come into the flat. The doorbell rang almost immediately afterwards and she assumed it was Priya's boyfriend, probably coming up to give her something she'd left behind in the car. She could hear Priya having a muffled conversation with someone on the landing—then footsteps came up to her door and someone tried the handle.

'Shweta?' Priya called out, knocking on the door.

'I've gone to bed!' Shweta yelled back. She knew she looked a fright—something like an avenging goddess on a bad hair day—and she didn't want Priya coming in and figuring out something was wrong.

'Nikhil's here,' Priya said.

Oh, great. That was all she needed—a scene in her flat in the middle of the night. She'd be lucky if the building's residents' society didn't turf them out—the society secretary had already started rumbling about male visitors not being allowed after eight p.m.

'I don't want to see him,' she said. 'Tell him to go away.'

Priya turned around and gave Nikhil a helpless look. She'd always had a soft spot for her flatmate's gorgeous boyfriend, and she thought Shweta was being completely unreasonable.

'Tell her I'm sorry,' he mouthed, and Priya relayed the message faithfully.

'He can go boil his head!' was the short and rather inelegant response.

Priya almost groaned aloud in despair. Of all the things to say! No wonder Shweta ended up with all the boring Siddhant types if this was the way she treated her men.

Nikhil's mouth was twitching with amusement, though—telling him to go boil his head sounded more like the fiery Shweta he knew than the ice maiden who'd put the phone down on him.

He'd realised he'd overstepped the mark the instant he'd made that remark about two-timing, and he was heartily sorry. He'd felt insanely jealous, though. He didn't believe for a moment that she had any feelings left for Siddhant, but the thought that she'd seriously considered marrying him when she wasn't even attracted to the man was a perpetual thorn in his side. It all boiled down to the same thing—Siddhant was eligible and he wasn't. Even if he did convince Shweta to marry him she'd always feel she'd settled for second-best. If he had any pride he'd give up on her, but the thought of spending the rest of his life without her was unbearable.

'Ask her if I can speak to her,' he said to Priya.

'No, he bloody well can't!' Shweta yelled from inside the room. 'Tell him to go away or I'll call the cops.'

There was silence outside the room for a few minutes, and then Shweta heard the front door shut. There was a tentative knock on her door, and Priya said, 'He's gone.'

'Good,' Shweta said grumpily. Shouting at Nikhil had lessened her anger somewhat—and in hindsight she could understand his being upset. Though she still couldn't see her way towards forgiving him for the accusation he'd made.

'Can I come in?'

'Are you sure he's gone? Because if he isn't I'll call your mom right now and tell her all about your boyfriend.'

'He's gone,' Priya said. 'Stop threatening me.'

Shweta got up and opened the door. Priya studied her carefully. 'You look like a homicidal maniac,' she said. 'Go and comb your hair, for heaven's sake. What was the hullabaloo about?'

'I had a fight with Nikhil,' Shweta said as she hunted for a comb.

Priya rolled her eyes in disgust. 'Really?' she said. 'Fancy that—I'd never have guessed.'

'He said I was two-timing him with Siddhant.'

'I did tell you that dinner was a bad idea,' Priya said. 'Though keeping loverboy on his toes isn't a bad strategy either. By the way, I don't think he's gone—I didn't hear his car start. He's got one of those expensive jobs, hasn't he? The engine sounds quite different. I noticed that when he pulled up in front of the building.'

Shweta went to the window. Sure enough, Nikhil's car was still there. She pulled the curtains together decisively.

'He can wait there all night if he wants,' she said. 'I'm not going to let him off so easily.'

Priya looked impressed. 'Remind me to take lessons from you on putting boyfriends in their place,' she said. 'That is if you still have a boyfriend at the end of this.'

Shweta was also privately beginning to wonder if Nikhil would still be around after the way she'd behaved. Perhaps she should let him in after all. Then his words came back to her and she stiffened her resolve. She hadn't asked him to wait outside—he should have listened to her and gone away for a while.

She drifted into an uneasy slumber after Priya left the room. Weird dreams plagued her, in which she ended up marrying Siddhant. Only at the last moment Siddhant slipped away, to be replaced by a giant alarm clock. After the fifth such dream she woke with a start. The luminous hands of her watch told her that it was three in the morning. Unable to stop herself, she got up and went to the window. Nikhil's car was still there.

'I give up!' she said in annoyance, and switched her phone on. Dialling Nikhil's number, she watched him as he sat up and took the call.

'Hey, Shweta,' he said.

His familiar voice sent little tendrils of longing through her. 'Why are you still here?'

'I'm not going until I get to see you and apologise,' he said. 'I was way out of line—I got jealous and lost my head.'

Shweta felt her resolve melt further at his admission. 'There was no reason for you to be jealous,' she said. 'If anything, I should be the one throwing jealous tantrums about you spending all your time with models and actresses.'

'I know. But what can I say? I'm not always rational.'

'Will you go home now?'

She couldn't see him clearly, but she could sense he was shaking his head. 'Not till I see you.'

'You'd better come up, then,' she said in resigned tones. 'You can't spend the whole night in your car.'

She went out and opened the front door. He was there in a few seconds. 'Your watchman was fast asleep,' he said as he came in. 'I don't think this place is very safe.'

'Well, I wouldn't have opened the door if you were a burglar,' Shweta said. 'Go into my room. I'll lock up and join you in a minute.'

He was sitting on her bed looking suitably contrite when she came in. 'I'm really sorry,' he said.

Shweta plumped down next to him. It was several days since they'd last been alone together, and her hands ached to touch him. It didn't help that he was looking particularly appealing—his hair had grown out a little and was flopping over his forehead in just the way she liked, and he was wearing a shirt in her favourite shade of midnight-blue. There was a slight stubble covering his face, and that added to his rather dangerous attractiveness.

'I can't handle anyone being controlling or possessive with me,' she said. 'My dad isn't possessive, but he's always been controlling—it took me years to break away from his influence, even after I'd grown up and left home. I'm not about to let myself be bossed around again, with you telling me whom I should meet and whom I shouldn't.'

'I understand,' he said, and it was clear he did. 'It won't happen again.'

It was getting more and more difficult to stay angry with him, and Shweta clenched her hands together in frustration.

'I don't even understand *why* you behaved the way you did!' she burst out. He raised his head, an arrested look on his face. 'I mean, I could have married Siddhant if I wanted to. *Why* would I dump him and start going around with you if it was him I wanted all along?'

Put that way, it was a difficult thing for him to explain—and in any case Nikhil wasn't sure he wanted to tell her everything.

'You were always thinking of *him* in terms of marriage,' he said, struggling to put at least part of his thoughts across without offending her. 'But marriage is the last thing on your mind as far as *I'm* concerned. I know you have your reasons. It's just a little…difficult to deal with at times.'

'You're a prize idiot,' Shweta said despairingly. 'Of *course* I was thinking marriage when I thought of Siddhant! I'm pushing thirty. I want to get married and have a family. I haven't ever had a serious relationship—all the men I know are good friends and not much else, and the few I've dated because I'm attracted to them turned out to be complete losers.'

'Didn't you consider an arranged marriage?' Nikhil was genuinely curious now—he'd never thought about the whole Siddhant thing from this angle before.

'There needs to be someone to do the arranging,' she said dryly. 'My father doesn't believe in arranged marriages, so a marriage of convenience seemed the best bet till you came along. *That's* why I was thinking of marrying Siddhant—he was pleasant enough, and he obviously wanted to marry me. And that's a rare combination, let me tell you.'

'Aren't *I* pleasant, then?' he asked, half-laughing, half-serious. Shweta looked into his eyes for a few seconds before getting onto her knees and leaning across to kiss him, slowly and lingeringly. It was the first time she'd had the opportunity to control a kiss in exactly the way she wanted—usually his reactions were so fast that she didn't get to explore fully, at her own pace. Now, however, he let her do as she liked, leaning back to give her better access as she unbuttoned his shirt and slid her hands across his chest, but not initiating anything himself. She gave a long sigh when she finally dragged her lips away from his.

'No, you're not pleasant,' she said. 'You're maddeningly attractive, and you make me want to throttle you and make love to you at the same time. Sometimes I think I won't be able to survive another minute if I don't have you. And you're there when I need you, and you're so thoughtful most of the time that I can't deal with it when you stop thinking and acting like an irrational idiot. So, no, you're not pleasant. But I love you all the same.'

'That's good enough for me,' he said, and there was a slight catch in his voice. 'Only I warn you—I'm not going to give up on convincing you to marry me.'

She put her arms around him, and this time he did respond, with a speed and suddenness that left her gasping for breath. Much later she thought that if he'd asked her to marry him at that instant she'd have agreed like a shot.

CHAPTER EIGHT

'WHY AREN'T YOU agreeing to get engaged?' Veena peered worriedly across the table at Shweta.

Nikhil was out of town for the day, and Shweta had offered to come over and spend time with Veena after work. Now, after ten minutes of being cross-examined by Veena on every possible aspect of her relationship with Nikhil, she was wishing she'd stayed back in the office.

'I'm not sure if he's really in love with me,' she said.

When they'd woken up the morning after they'd made up he'd turned to her and said, 'You know, you're the only person I know who's been really, really angry with me multiple times and hasn't ended up calling me an illegitimate bastard.'

Evidently he thought that was the ultimate proof of her goodness as a human being, and that had further confirmed her opinion on why he wanted to marry her. He might not be conscious of it himself, but he felt that he was safe with her—she knew everything about him, and she accepted him the way he was. In Delhi he'd told her that the only girl he'd been in a long-term relationship with had broken off with him when she found out he was illegitimate. He'd made a joke of the incident, but Shweta couldn't help feeling that it had affected him badly. And the facts spoke for themselves—since then he'd had one meaningless fling after another.

'I don't know why you think that,' Veena was saying. 'He's crazy about you. He can't stop singing your praises.'

Shweta sighed. This was why she hadn't wanted to come. She didn't like discussing Nikhil with anyone—and especially not his stepmother. She wasn't even sure why she was holding out, not agreeing to marry Nikhil, when every cell in her brain was crying out to her to say yes. For the last few days she had been wondering if she'd made a mistake—Nikhil had displayed every sign of being deeply in love with her.

'It's complicated,' she said finally.

Veena stayed silent for a while, then she asked diffidently, 'Does Nikhil talk about his parents?'

'Not much,' Shweta said, feeling more and more uncomfortable. 'I get the impression he's not on good terms with them.'

'No, he quarrelled very badly with his father when he visited us last. But I know his father would forgive him if he just made the first move—called him up, or visited us in Kerala.'

'From what I understand, Nikhil thinks it's his father who needs forgiving,' Shweta said sharply.

Veena looked even more distressed. 'He doesn't understand… It's my fault. I should speak to him, but it's so difficult…'

'I don't think it's your fault at all,' Shweta told her. 'Let's talk of something else, Veena Aunty. I don't think Nikhil would be very happy if he knew we were discussing his parents.'

Veena changed the topic, but after dinner she came back to it again. 'Shweta, I know you think you shouldn't get involved, but it would help so much if you could speak to Nikhil once. He'll listen to you—he cuts me off every time I bring up the topic.'

Privately Shweta thought that Nikhil would cut her off as well—and a lot more rudely. Persuading Veena of this was way beyond her powers, though, and Shweta found herself agreeing to try and speak to him.

At least one person seemed happy, she thought gloomily as she left the flat—Veena was beaming. Clearly she thought Shweta would have everything sorted in no time.

Nikhil got back to Mumbai the next day, and he called her almost as soon as he landed.

'Can you get out of the office a little early today?' he asked. 'I thought we could meet up for a drink after work and you could come over for dinner with us afterwards—I was planning to order in so Amma gets a break from cooking.'

For once Shweta wasn't looking forward to meeting him, and she almost chickened out before better sense prevailed. Given that she'd been stupid enough to promise Veena that she'd speak to Nikhil, she might as well get it done with.

'I can leave by six,' she said. Deepa was out for a meeting, and it was best to leave before she got back.

'Great. I'll pick you up from outside your office.' He paused, then said softly, 'I've missed you.'

'Umm…me too,' Shweta said self-consciously.

There were multiple disadvantages to working in an open office—not least of which was everyone around her being able to hear what she was saying. She rang off as soon as she could, and went back to work—she'd dawdled a bit in the first half of the day, and would have to work like a beaver to be done by six.

Nikhil took her to a rooftop lounge bar in a swanky new hotel—thirty-four floors up, it had an amazing view of the Mumbai skyline on one side and the sea on the other.

The wind whipped at Shweta's hair, and she grimaced a little as she sat down next to him on an elegant black sofa.

'Don't you like it?' Nikhil asked.

'Oh, I do,' she said. 'It's just that if I'd known we were coming here I'd have dressed up a little.'

She was wearing a lime-green cotton *salwar kameez*, with matching leather slippers. Everyone else was in Western clothes, and there were a fair number of foreigners around. Nikhil himself was wearing an expensive-looking jacket over jeans and a white linen shirt, and his shoes looked as if they were designer-made.

His gaze softened as he looked at her. Her cheeks had turned pink and her hair was tousled by the breeze. She'd never looked prettier.

'You look perfect,' he said. 'I like you better in regular clothes than when you're dressed up with make-up on.'

Given that she'd spent a frantic ten minutes in the office loo, trying to do her face, that didn't say much for her make-up skills, but Shweta laughed.

'That's because you're used to hobnobbing with actresses and models all the time,' she said. 'It's a relief being with a frump.'

'You're not a frump.' Nikhil leaned across and touched her face lightly. 'I always thought you were beautiful—even when you were in school and wore those hideous glasses with black plastic frames.'

Shweta put her head to one side. 'That's a bit difficult to believe,' she said. 'Sure you aren't brainwashing yourself? Telling yourself you've always loved me and that it was fate, meeting me again…?'

'I'm sure,' he said, and tipped her face up to drop a kiss on her lips.

Shweta squirmed away—she was conservative enough to feel uncomfortable about kissing in public. 'Don't,' she said. 'There are other people around.'

He moved away a little and gave her an indulgent smile. 'You're cute when you're embarrassed,' he said.

'I'm even cuter when I wallop people with my handbag,' she retorted. 'And that's what going to happen to you if you try kissing me again.'

'I have a violent girlfriend,' Nikhil informed the server who'd just come up with their drinks. 'If you see blood pouring out of my head you'll know I've just been savagely attacked by her.'

'Yes, sir,' the man said gravely.

Shweta went scarlet. 'He's joking,' she said.

'Yes, ma'am.'

'And there aren't any oranges in my sangria. Only enough apples to make a pie with.'

He peered into her glass. 'I'm sorry, ma'am. I'll let the bartender know. I think the recipe we use doesn't have oranges in it. Can I offer you something else instead?'

'No, it doesn't matter.'

She looked so disappointed that Nikhil laughed.

'Why are you so stuck on the oranges?' he asked when the server had gone away. 'I think you injured that poor man's pride, finding fault with his recipe.'

Shweta glared at him. 'You'll be the one injured if you make any more stupid remarks. And a lot more than just your pride.'

Nikhil laughed and threw up his hands in surrender. 'I'm sorry…I'm sorry. Couldn't resist it.'

Slightly mollified, Shweta sat back and sipped at her drink. She'd had sangria for the first time in Spain, and loved the way they made it there. It just didn't taste as good without the oranges, but it would sound silly and pretentious to say so.

She was wondering how to broach the topic of his parents with Nikhil when she saw him take a jewellery box out of his pocket.

'I got you something,' he said.

He clicked the box open and there, nestled in black velvet, was a pair of exquisite diamond earrings. They matched the ring he'd given her earlier, and in the evening light the diamonds sparkled with all the colours of the setting sun.

'They're lovely,' she said. 'Thank you, Nikhil!' Taking them out of the box, she slid them into her ears.

Nikhil watched her and said, 'I wish you'd done the same with the ring.'

She was about to give a flippant reply, but there was something in his voice that stopped her. 'Nikhil—I've only asked for some more time,' she said helplessly.

He met her gaze squarely. 'You can have all the time you need. I'm not trying to pressure you into saying yes. It's just that sometimes—well, sometimes I wish I didn't have to wait.'

There was a short pause and Shweta kept on looking at him, scanning his eyes keenly. She'd come very close to agreeing to the engagement twice before, but doubts had held her back. Now she was almost a hundred percent sure that Nikhil was in love with her—the doubts were probably stemming from her own lack of self-confidence. There were risks, of course. Nikhil would never make a safe or comfortable husband, and with his lifestyle he would always be surrounded by women a dozen times more attractive than her. But which was better? Taking the risk of having her heart broken some years down the line, or making sure she got it broken right away by breaking up with him?

Nikhil looked away first. 'I'm sorry,' he said. 'This is way too heavy for evening conversation.' He picked up the jewellery box and put her old earrings into it, held the box out to her. 'Here—maybe you should put these away before you lose them.'

As she took the box from him she noticed that his hands were shaking a little—and his lips were compressed, as if he was suppressing a strong emotion with some difficulty.

'Have you got the ring with you?' she asked.

Nikhil's eyes flew to her face. He shook his head, but his eyes were ablaze with hope. 'I'm a little superstitious about carrying it,' he said. 'Does this mean…?'

'It means, yes—I'd love to marry you,' Shweta said. Nikhil promptly pulled her into his arms and did his best to kiss her senseless. Shweta emerged from his arms a few minutes later with her hair tumbled and cheeks aflame.

'I told you not to kiss me in front of other people,' she muttered, but she wasn't really angry this time.

Nikhil looked completely unrepentant. 'Special circumstances,' he said. His eyes were sparkling with devilry and he looked magnificent, with sunlight glinting off the angles of his perfectly sculpted face and his lean, strong body draped across the sofa.

'You know, this is a pretty nice hotel,' he said. 'What do you say to checking into one of the rooms and celebrating our engagement properly?'

It sounded too tempting for words, but Shweta frowned in mock annoyance. 'Absolutely not,' she said. 'We're not officially engaged until you give me the ring anyway. And I want to finish my drink.'

Nikhil watched her sip at the drink. Under his scrutiny she grew more and more conscious, finally spilling a bit onto her clothes.

'Stop it,' she said, swatting at his hand as he leaned

forward and mopped at the stain with a spotless handkerchief. 'You're doing it on purpose—looking at me like that.'

'Like what?' he asked innocently, leaning back in his chair. 'Can't I even look at my fiancée?'

His eyes were dancing with unholy glee and Shweta frowned at him. 'You know exactly what I mean,' she chided. 'Let's talk about something else.'

'There *was* something I wanted to ask you, actually,' Nikhil said, and his abrupt switch to a serious tone made her look up in surprise. 'Would you object if Amma came and lived here in Mumbai?'

'I thought she didn't want to move?'

'I'm going to convince her,' Nikhil said, and there was a confident smile on his lips. 'I was originally going to ask her to move into my flat, but now I think it would work better for all of us if I get her another apartment in the same building.'

It was the perfect opening, and in spite of her misgivings Shweta took it.

'Veena Aunty's not going to move here until you sort things out with your dad,' she said. 'She's spoken to me a couple of times about it.'

Nikhil frowned. 'I thought I told you—my father and I aren't on speaking terms any more.'

'That's exactly what's upsetting Veena Aunty. Look, I don't want to interfere, but for my sake just give her a fair hearing, OK? I won't bring the topic up again afterwards.'

'I'll speak to her,' Nikhil said. 'But right now I'm calling for the bill, and then we're heading to my office so that I can retrieve the ring. I knew it was a good sign, finding those matching earrings.'

'Yes, of course—*that's* why I agreed to marry you,' Shweta said. 'So that I could get a ring to match my earrings.'

He laughed. 'I'm too worried that might be true to ask questions,' he said. 'I know how important it is for you to have matching accessories.' He looked pointedly at her lime-green slippers and bag, and Shweta made a face. 'But let's come back here after we get the ring—I do want to celebrate properly.'

As it turned out they didn't end up going back—Nikhil remembered that the ring was in his flat, and that Veena was there, waiting for them for dinner.

'OK if I tell her?' Nikhil asked in an undertone when they reached his apartment. 'I'm sorry about this. I completely forgot that she was here, that I'd even told her we'd come back for dinner.'

'You told me,' Shweta said, suppressing a smile. It was rather endearing, his having forgotten all the plans he'd made for the evening just because she'd agreed to marry him. 'Let's tell her—and let's celebrate by ordering in the most expensive meal possible.'

To say that Veena was over the moon was an understatement. She hovered over Shweta and made gushing remarks and generally got in the way, but it was impossible to be annoyed with her because she was so genuinely happy. The only sour note was introduced when she asked Nikhil when he would tell his parents.

'I'm not planning to speak to them,' he said shortly. 'You can tell them if you want.'

Veena shot Shweta an appealing look, but Shweta didn't want to interfere in something that Nikhil evidently felt strongly about. She changed the topic and Veena followed her lead, though a worried frown still puckered her forehead.

Nikhil was just dropping Shweta back home, and she looked at him in surprise when he pulled the car over halfway between their apartments. 'Something wrong with the car?' she asked.

He shook his head. 'No, there's something wrong with me,' he said, leaning over her to release her seat belt and pull her into his arms. 'I'm likely to die of frustration,' he muttered against her lips as he began to kiss her. 'We should have checked into that hotel, and to hell with everybody else.'

The kiss was explosive, and when they finally broke apart Shweta found herself trembling.

'We're likely to get pulled in by the cops for indecent behaviour in public,' she said shakily. 'Let's go.'

Priya had some friends over, and Nikhil refused to come upstairs. He knew Shweta well enough to know that she'd feel awkward and embarrassed taking him into her room if other people were around.

'I'll see you soon,' he said, caressing her face.

Even the gentlest touch had the capacity to send her up in flames, and for a second she was tempted to forget her scruples and drag Nikhil up to her flat. Then she remembered Veena, and how scandalised she would be if Nikhil stayed the night with Shweta. Sighing, she stepped back and waved as Nikhil got into his dangerous-looking car and drove away.

Shweta spent the next day in a happy daze. So far she'd only told Priya about the engagement. Her father and aunt would need to be told soon, but Shweta wanted to tell them face to face. She was slightly apprehensive about her father's reaction. In spite of having finally broken away from her father's overpowering influence, she found herself regressing a bit now, when it came to her marriage—she wanted him to approve.

It was around seven in the morning on Saturday when her phone rang, and for a few seconds Shweta didn't recognise the agitated female voice. When she finally realised who it was, she said, 'Veena Aunty, you need to calm down—I can't understand a word of what you're saying.'

'I need to come and see you. Can you message me your address? I'll take a taxi and come.'

'What's happened? Is Nikhil OK?'

'Yes, yes, Nikhil is fine. But he's very upset with me, and I really need to see you before I leave.'

'Leave for where?' Shweta asked in bewilderment. Only the day before Nikhil had told her that Veena might be staying on for another week, to meet some distant relatives from the US who were passing through Mumbai.

'I'm leaving for Kerala today. Nikhil's father has booked the tickets. I just need to go to the airport and pick them up, he said. But I have an hour or two, and I need to speak to you.'

Shweta could get nothing more concrete out of Veena on the phone, and finally gave her detailed directions to her apartment. When she arrived Veena seemed a lot

more composed than she'd sounded over the phone—
only the way she was twisting her *sari pallu* betrayed
how upset she was.

'Why is Nikhil angry?' Shweta asked gently.

'I asked him to tell his parents about the engagement and he refused. Maybe I should have let it go, but
I thought it was important for him to call them—and
they will need to be involved in the preparations for
the wedding... Your father would think it very strange
if they didn't participate. Then Nikhil said he wasn't
even planning to invite them.'

Clearly that statement had led Veena to remonstrate
with him, and their argument had got completely out of
hand, with Nikhil storming out of the house at the end
of it. While Shweta sympathised with Veena, she could
see the whole thing from Nikhil's point of view as well.

'He hasn't really forgiven them for all he went
through when he was growing up,' she said gently. 'It
couldn't have been easy, dealing with all the gossip
around his being illegitimate.'

'If he wasn't illegitimate he wouldn't exist,' Veena
said. 'Better being illegitimate than not being born.'

As a statement, it was a difficult one to argue against,
but Shweta was finding it incredible that Veena, who
had far greater cause for complaint than Nikhil, was
staunchly defending her husband.

'I think he feels that his dad was very unfair to you.'

'He doesn't know anything about it,' Veena said. 'It's
I who wasn't fair to Nikhil's father. He's always been a
perfect gentleman.'

OK, this was really strange. Shweta gave up on trying to understand. Her face must have reflected her confusion, because after a pause Veena said with great difficulty, 'I could never be a proper wife to Nikhil's father.'

'Because you couldn't have children?'

'No, that's not what I mean. We never—never lived together like man and wife.'

Never living together *like man and wife* was presumably a euphemism for *we never had sex*, and Shweta finally began to understand. Not sure how to respond, she asked tentatively, 'So, was that because of a medical issue?'

Veena shook her head. 'Not a medical problem. It's not a very...*nice* story. I'm going to tell you, though—that's the only way to make you understand.' She waited till Shweta nodded in assent, and then continued. 'I grew up in a family in Kerala. My parents were very simple folk—they had a farm, and my father was out on the farm most of the day. My mother would be busy with the cooking and the housework and the younger children. I was the oldest and I had three younger brothers.'

She paused a little, and Shweta wondered where the story was going.

Veena continued, 'There was a distant cousin of my father's who used to come home often. He was a college graduate, but he was unemployed. He told my mother he would help me with my studies...'

And then Shweta knew. It was the kind of story she'd read in magazines and books and been horrified by—hearing Veena talk about it in her flat monotone was sickening in a more gruesomely immediate way, even couched in euphemisms.

'He misbehaved with me—I was only nine...' It was a heart-rending story.

'I'm so sorry,' Shweta said, and the words sounded pathetically inadequate. 'I can't imagine how you would have felt... Didn't you tell anyone?'

'I was scared,' Veena said, and smiled briefly. 'It was too shameful to talk about. And my mother was always so busy. It went on for three years, until I turned twelve and became a woman.'

Became a woman was a common way of describing reaching puberty, and Shweta didn't ask for an explanation.

'And then you married Nikhil's father?'

'It was an arranged marriage—my father chose the groom for me. Nikhil's father was well-educated, and he lived in Pune. I wanted to get away from the village.'

Shweta noted that, like most ultra-conservative women, Veena didn't call her husband by name—'Nikhil's father' was the term she always used. Irrelevantly Shweta wondered what Veena had called him through the ten years before Nikhil was born.

'How old were you when you married?'

'Nineteen. At first Nikhil's father thought I was just shy and scared, because I was so young. Then he realised that something was wrong.'

'And you told him?'

Veena shook her head. 'He guessed. He asked who the man was. I couldn't talk about it. I never have. This is the first time I've—' She broke off and her face contorted with grief. 'Nikhil's father was so good to me. He was like a brother to me after that. I felt terrible— he was a young man and I was ruining his life. I could never have his children…'

'And then he met Ranjini Aunty?'

'We'd been married for ten years. He never reproached me. If I tried to apologise all he would say was that it wasn't my fault. But I knew he wanted a proper family—not a wife in name only who cooked and cleaned… And then he met Ranjini. He didn't want to hurt me, but they fell in love. They never wanted to tell me. It was only when they found out that there was going to be a baby that Nikhil's father came and told me. Even then he said that Ranjini would move to a different city and he would send money to look after the child…'

'You asked him to bring her home instead?'

'Yes.' Veena tried to smile. 'Nowadays it would be a lot simpler—I would have a job, and I could divorce him so that he could marry Ranjini instead. But I had no job, only a high school education, and I couldn't stand the thought of going back to my village. My parents would have died of shame. And I wanted to see a baby in the house—I wanted Nikhil's father to watch his son grow up.'

A thought struck Shweta. 'Was the man still there? In your village?'

Veena shook her head. 'He died in a motorcycle accident soon after I got married. So at least I didn't have to see him when I went home on visits. And I don't think he misbehaved with any other girls—he had begun to drink, and people stopped allowing him into their homes.'

There was a short pause while Shweta digested what she'd just been told.

Then Veena said, 'Nikhil isn't really illegitimate.'

'But I thought you said a divorce wasn't possible?'

'Not then. But around the time Nikhil got expelled from school we were shifting cities anyway, so his father and I filed for divorce by mutual consent. Ranjini and his father married soon after the divorce was finalised.'

Shweta stared at her. 'But why haven't you told Nikhil this?' she asked. 'It would make things so much easier for him!'

'He knows,' Veena said sadly. 'He was the first person we told. It made him settle down for a while, but then he started brooding about it and he turned very bitter. You see, he was always very attached to me. Both his parents were working, and I'd looked after him for most of his growing up years—I'd always loved children, and maybe I even spoilt him a bit. I was so worried about people misunderstanding, thinking I was ill-treating him because he was my husband's illegitimate child... At some point he started blaming his parents. He thought they had coerced me into agreeing to the divorce. Nothing I could say would convince him.'

'He's never told me about this,' Shweta said in a daze. 'And we've discussed it a lot. He even told me he was upset because his dad and mom are "pretending" to be married.'

'That's what he said to them as well. The last time he

was home he had a terrible fight with his father. And he got so angry yesterday, when I tried to convince him to make up with them… I can't stay with him any more. I feel like I've stolen Ranjini's son away from her.'

Shweta sat silently for a while, trying to absorb what she'd heard. She felt sorriest for Nikhil's father—to be vilified by his own son for a sin he hadn't really committed seemed grossly unfair.

'Do you want me to tell him—tell Nikhil, I mean?'

Veena shook her head in panic. 'No! I can't bear the thought of him knowing—he's more than a son to me. It would kill me, having him know what happened to me.'

Shweta stared at her in frustration. 'He'd understand, Veena Aunty, and he wouldn't mention it to you ever! It's the only solution—can't you see?'

Veena shook her head again. 'It would kill me,' she repeated. 'Promise me you won't tell him.'

When Shweta hesitated, she said, 'You have to promise me. Otherwise I'll need to cut off all ties between me and Nikhil.'

Which would only make matters worse. And in any case, whatever she might feel about it, the secret was not hers to share. Reluctantly, Shweta promised not to breathe a word to Nikhil.

'But what do you want me to do, then? What was the point of telling me this if you don't want me to tell Nikhil?'

'Convince him to come and meet his father,' Veena said. 'To reconcile with him. If his father wants to tell him part of the story I won't say anything. But Nikhil needs to make the first move.'

'So far my trying to convince him has been pretty disastrous,' Shweta said. 'But I'll try once again if you want.'

It was getting late, and Shweta called a cab to drop Veena to the airport. She even offered to come with her and help her get her ticket from the airlines, but Veena refused.

'I've troubled you enough today,' she said, giving Shweta a grateful kiss on the forehead. 'God bless you, child. I'm sure Nikhil will listen to you.'

Marvelling at Veena's completely misplaced confidence in her, Shweta waved her goodbye. Then she looked down at the ring on her finger, twisting it around a couple of times with a wry smile on her lips. She'd have to speak to Nikhil, but given a choice between bringing up the topic with him and getting a root canal treatment, she'd choose the root canal any day. Perhaps even without anaesthetic.

CHAPTER NINE

'THE LEAST YOU could do is hear me out!'

Nikhil said steadily, 'I've heard enough. Shweta, I hate to say this, but you have no idea of what you're talking about.'

'But you're not even illegitimate! Your parents got married, didn't they?'

'Yes, they did—but that's not the point. They coerced Amma into agreeing to the divorce.'

Shweta gave him an exasperated look. 'She was an adult woman! You can't force someone into a divorce like that. Does it never occur to you that she might have had her own reasons for agreeing?'

As soon as she said it Shweta realised that she was skating a little too close to the truth.

Nikhil was shaking his head, and though he sounded quite calm when he spoke a vein was throbbing in his temple. 'Yes, she *did* have her reasons. She had no job, and she was from a poor and terribly conservative family—they wouldn't have taken her back if my dad had thrown her out. She'd have probably starved on the streets!'

'Nikhil, I've met your dad. And I've heard Veena Aunty talk about him so much. There's no way you can make me believe that he forced her into a divorce.'

'Perhaps it wasn't that, then. Perhaps it was me.'

'Perhaps it was you, what? *You* threatened to throw her out?'

Nikhil shook his head. 'No. Maybe you're right, my dad would have supported her financially, but she'd never have seen me again—she had no rights over me. I wasn't related to her. Maybe that's what she couldn't deal with. She was barren herself, but she loved children. She'd looked after me all my life and she had no other real family. Even her parents were dead by then, and she wasn't very close to her brothers.'

If Shweta hadn't known it to be untrue, it would have seemed a very plausible story. For a second she wondered if she should just let the topic rest. She couldn't help remembering Veena's tortured expression, though, and in spite of her better judgement she ploughed on. 'Nikhil, it's stuff that's between *them*. You'll never know what really happened. Why don't you take them at face value? Veena Aunty's obviously happy with them, or she would have agreed to come and live with you.'

Nikhil asked abruptly, 'Why are you so interested in me making up with my parents all of a sudden?'

'I told you! Veena Aunty came to me and she was upset—I'm trying to help. But the more I speak to you, the more convinced I am that it's utterly useless trying to talk sense into your thick head.'

'And from what I can figure, Amma's worried that

your father will say no to the wedding if my parents aren't involved at every stage. I can't think where she would have got the idea other than from you,' he said.

The thought that she was ashamed of his background had been eating at him from the day they'd started dating. Shweta still hadn't told her father that they were engaged. He'd told himself that he would give her time, but in the face of her insistence that he reconcile with his parents it was difficult not to flare up at her.

'I've *never* spoken to her about what my father might say!' Shweta exclaimed. 'Really, Nikhil, you're pushing it a bit too far. Even if my father said no, that wouldn't stop me from marrying you.'

Nikhil shrugged, his eyes remote. 'Your father will hate the thought of us marrying, won't he?'

Shweta hesitated. She wasn't really sure how her father would react—she suspected he wouldn't be very pleased, but explaining to Nikhil in his current mood that her father had rigid views on most things and rarely approved of her decisions would be difficult.

'I'm not sure,' she said finally. 'It doesn't really matter, does it?'

He didn't answer.

Shweta said, '*Does* it, Nikhil?'

'It doesn't matter to me,' Nikhil said slowly. 'I know you keep saying you're out of your dad's shadow, but you're always trying to live up to his expectations.'

'What?'

'Now that you've found out that my parents are married after all you want me to reconcile with them, so that you can present a nice textbook family to your father. Reformed son, reasonably successful, legally married parents...'

Shweta stared at him for a few seconds, and then anger began to kick in. 'If I cared about any of that I wouldn't have got involved with you to begin with!' she said. 'I could have gone ahead and married Siddhant, or someone like that. Why would I bother getting engaged to *you*?'

There was another short pause, and then Nikhil said, 'I guess it helps that you actually enjoy sleeping with me.'

His voice wasn't even cold, it was matter-of-fact, and somehow that made it worse.

'You don't have a very high opinion of me, do you?' Shweta asked, fighting to keep her voice steady.

'I could say the same of you,' Nikhil said.

Quite suddenly, Shweta knew she'd had enough. Nikhil didn't trust her, and there was nothing she could say that would make a difference. It was ironic, really— given the number of relationships he'd had in the past, *she* was the one with a logical reason not to trust *him*.

'Maybe we should take a break from each other,' she said, and she was surprised at how calm she sounded. Jumbled thoughts were warring for attention in her mind—one part of her was grappling with a deep sense of hurt, while another was wondering whether she was going completely mad.

Nikhil had gone very still. 'Just because I won't listen to you and go running to my parents?'

She bit her lip. It wasn't that. It was because he didn't trust her, and because she still wasn't sure if he really loved her. At that point if Nikhil had made the slightest move towards her she would have probably collapsed gratefully into his arms. He didn't, though—he just kept looking at her, his expression grim.

'Not just that,' she said finally. 'I'm not sure you're really committed to us being together. It's just convenient because you've known me for so long, and…and because I know about your family and everything.'

There—she'd said it.

His face was like granite, but she floundered on. 'We don't really have much in common. I don't move in the same circles as you do, I wouldn't fit in with all your celebrity friends, and you'd get bored with me after a while.'

'Spare me,' he said. 'I've used the "it's-not-you-it's-me" line too often to be fooled by it. We'll take a break, then, if that's what you want.' When she didn't answer, he said, 'Let me know when you're ready to give it a go again.'

Shweta nodded silently and Nikhil turned towards the door. Halfway there, he turned back, and Shweta felt a ridiculous surge of hope go through her. His eyes were still grim, though, and the hope died as quickly as it had been born.

'If we do get back together it has to be on the understanding that you don't try interfering in parts of my life that don't concern you,' he said, and his voice was hard and uncompromising.

'I'll try to remember that—if I'm ever tempted to get back with you,' Shweta said hotly.

He shrugged. 'Always better to make things clear.'

Shweta suddenly saw red. Despite what he'd said, he seemed so *sure* that she'd come crawling back to him. Rather as if she was a child throwing an unnecessary tantrum. He wasn't even acknowledging that they had a genuine problem, preferring instead to believe that she was splitting up with him because she was ashamed of his parentage.

Deliberately she took the diamond engagement ring off her finger and tugged the matching earrings out of her ears.

'Maybe you should take these with you,' she said, her voice icy-cold. 'Just in case I don't change my mind.'

Something changed in Nikhil's face and Shweta knew that she'd done something that couldn't be easily undone. For a few seconds she stared into his eyes, her expression defiant as she held out the jewellery.

'Sell the stuff if you don't change your mind,' he said and, turning around, he strode out of the room without another word.

The rest of the day was hell for her. Unable to cry, she paced the room, replaying the things Nikhil had said over and over in her head. What he'd said had revealed a lot about the way he thought of her. Perhaps there were excuses that could be made for him—she was in no frame of mind to make them. All she could think was that she'd been right all along when she'd believed he didn't love her.

'I need a week off,' she told Deepa the next day.

She'd expected Deepa to create trouble. The sleepless night had, however, left dark circles under her eyes, and she looked only inches away from a nervous breakdown.

Deepa took one look at her and nodded briskly. 'Sure,' she said. 'Hand over your work to Faisal. He owes you for picking up the slack when he broke his wrist. Do you want to take off from tomorrow or Monday?'

'Tomorrow, please,' Shweta said.

She left the room without remembering to thank Deepa, and the other man in the room raised his eyebrows.

'Getting soft in your old age, Deepa?' he asked.

She laughed and shook her head. 'Shweta's a good resource,' she said. 'And Diwali's coming up anyway, so work is slack. Something must have happened—she's behaving very uncharacteristically.'

'Boyfriend trouble?'

'Isn't it always? And in this case the boyfriend is a hotshot type. Sometimes I feel thankful I'm middle-aged and married and beyond all this.'

Shweta would have given a lot to be beyond heartbreak, but unfortunately there wasn't a switch she could turn off to stop the hurt. Mechanically, she took Faisal through the documents on the audit she was currently handling.

'Is everything OK?' he ventured once she was done. 'You look upset.'

Shweta made an effort to pull herself together. 'Everything's fine,' she said. 'I just need a break. Now, are you sure you've got all that?'

'I think so,' Faisal said. 'You're still in town, right?

Or are you going to Pune? I might need to call you if I get stuck.'

Until he mentioned it Shweta hadn't thought of going to Pune, but now that the idea had presented itself it seemed the logical thing to do.

'I'll probably leave tomorrow,' she said. 'I haven't seen my dad in a while.'

She booked her bus tickets online before she left the office. Nikhil had tried calling her once, and she half expected him to be waiting for her when she got back home. There was no sign of his gleaming black car, though. Not sure whether she was disappointed or relieved, she climbed the stairs to her second-floor flat. It didn't take long to pack, and for the sake of something to do she clicked on the TV.

She was flipping channels when she came across a live telecast of a Bollywood awards show. Award shows were a dime a dozen now, and she vaguely remembered Nikhil talking about this particular one with her. Perhaps that was what made her stay tuned to the channel, blankly watching a lissom starlet gyrating around the stage with a troupe of bare-chested male dancers. The number came to an end and the starlet ran off the stage to thunderous applause. Anjalika Arora came onto the stage next, and Shweta sat up.

Anjalika looked stunning, in a gold sequinned sari with a halterneck blouse. She was heavily made-up, and even under the glaring lights she looked a good ten years younger than she actually was—the young debutant actor next to her was completely overshadowed. They were speaking into the microphones alternately—a carefully rehearsed but impromptu-sounding conversation, full of innuendo and Bollywood in-jokes. Anjalika announced the next set of awards and stepped off the stage. The camera followed her as she went back to her seat in the audience, and with a jolt Shweta realised who she was sitting next to. *Nikhil.* In a perfectly cut evening suit, with his hair gelled back, he looked remote and rather grim. The camera stayed focussed on him for a few seconds, and Shweta found herself hungrily taking in every detail of his appearance.

In spite of telling herself that she was being stupid, Shweta stayed glued to the TV until the programme came to an end. They didn't show Nikhil or Anjalika again, and she found herself wondering if they'd left together. Then she shook herself in annoyance. Nikhil's job entailed attending events of this sort—from what he'd said, he didn't even like them much—but they helped him build contacts that would be useful for his business. And surely it was unfair expecting him to stay home and brood when Shweta herself had been the one to split up with him.

It was five in the morning when she got out of bed after a largely sleepless night. It took her less than half an hour to bathe and change. She'd planned to have breakfast before she left, but her appetite had almost completely deserted her.

The bus route to Pune was one she had taken so often that she hardly registered the spectacular view of the Western Ghats as the bus zipped down the expressway. She couldn't stop thinking of Nikhil, of the expression on his face when she'd asked him to go. Slowly she was beginning to question her own behaviour. Shouldn't she have paused a little? Tried to understand *why* he'd come up with the ridiculous idea that she was ashamed of him? Quite likely it was something she'd said or done that had given him the impression. And instead of waiting till they'd both had a chance to calm down she'd given him back his ring.

Her father was waiting for her at the bus stop in his battered old Fiat. It was the same car he'd used for the last fifteen years, and nothing would convince him that he should upgrade.

'You needn't have come to pick me up,' Shweta said, the way she did every time.

So far it hadn't deterred Dr Mathur from driving down to the bus station whenever she was expected. He took her bag from her and put it in the boot—with a pang, Shweta noticed that his movements were slower than last time. Though in excellent health, Dr Mathur was growing old.

'How's Anita Bua doing?' Shweta's aunt never came to pick her up—instead she stayed at home, cooking up a storm to greet her niece.

'Looking forward to seeing you,' her father said. 'It's been a while since you last visited us.'

He was right—ever since Nikhil had arrived on the scene Shweta had reduced her visits to Pune. She'd told herself that it was because her father and aunt had their own fairly busy lives to lead, because she needed to get out of the habit of running to Pune every time she felt lonely. For the first time it occurred to her that they might have missed her.

'I've been busy,' she said, trying not to sound defensive. 'But I'm here for a week now.'

Her father gave her a quick look—which she missed, being lost in her own thoughts. He didn't say anything. Shweta's aunt, on the other hand, was a lot more vocal.

'Are you ill, child?' she asked, the second she set eyes on Shweta. 'You've got dark circles under your eyes and you don't look half as bouncy as you normally do.'

Shweta winced at 'bouncy'. She didn't feel as if she would even want to smile any time in the foreseeable future—being asked to bounce was almost an unforgivable insult.

'She has a demanding job,' her father said, wheeling her suitcase into the house. 'Let her relax for a while. She probably doesn't want to be bombarded with questions.' But when Shweta had left the room he raised his eyebrows enquiringly at his sister.

'Something's happened,' Anita said, unconsciously echoing Deepa's reaction when she'd seen Shweta the day before. 'I've never seen her like this before.'

Dr Mathur just grunted in response, but Anita knew him too well to be miffed. Even Shweta herself probably didn't realise how much he cared for her.

After a day or so Shweta began to look a little less distraught. Her heart still ached when she thought of Nikhil, and a couple of times she almost broke down and called him. But being around her father and aunt helped. Neither of them were demonstrative people, but they cared for her deeply, and having them around was helping to centre her and make her think more calmly.

Nikhil not having called her was proof in her mind that he'd decided a break-up was the best option. Pride stopped her from making the first move, and as the days went by she was feeling more and more resigned to the possibility that she might never get back with Nikhil.

'Dad, do you remember Mr Nair?' she asked one day, in what she hoped was a casual manner. Dr Mathur was puttering around in the garden, and he carefully finished watering his roses before he answered.

'The building contractor?'

'Yes, he…um…had a son who was in my class in school.'

'Nikhil? I remember him. Felt rather sorry for the boy—he had a lot to deal with. Got expelled from school finally, didn't he?'

Shweta gaped at him. 'Weren't you on the board then? I thought *you* decided to expel him.'

'It was a board decision,' Shweta's father said, frowning. 'He'd been caught smoking on the school premises, and there had been other disciplinary issues earlier. We didn't have much of a choice. But we did call the father down to the school and advise him to take the boy in hand. And we issued a transfer certificate instead of an expulsion letter when he told us that they were moving out of Pune. Why the sudden interest?'

He was looking right at her, and despite herself, Shweta began to blush. 'I ran into him recently,' she said. 'He's doing quite well—runs a large event management company.'

'I'm not surprised. He had a lot of potential even when he was in school.'

Dr Mathur seemed to lose interest in the subject as he examined a fat caterpillar basking on one of his roses. When Shweta went indoors, however, he looked up. There was a thoughtful look in his eyes that his sister would have recognised.

Once inside, Shweta switched on the TV and began flipping channels. It was an indication of the depths of her desperation that she actually tuned in to the channel that had been screening the awards show, in the hope that they would do a re-run. Seeing Nikhil on TV would be better than not seeing him at all. The channel, however, was running a soap of the warring in-laws variety, and she switched the TV off in disgust.

It would probably have made her feel a lot better if she'd known that Nikhil was in as bad, if not worse shape. He'd spent the days immediately after their quarrel trying to whip up his anger against Shweta. Then slowly dull resignation had begun to settle in. The more he thought about it, the more convinced he was that Shweta's hesitation in getting engaged, and her later insistence on his contacting his parents, had to do with the fact that she was ashamed of his background. Except he could no longer summon up the will to be indignant about it—at times he even found himself thinking that she was right.

The switch from anger to depression made his spirits sink completely. He was sure he still wanted Shweta—whatever else he was confused about, that fact stood out clear and incontrovertible. He'd tried visiting Shweta's apartment, to talk her around, but Priya had told him that Shweta was in Pune for a week. She didn't volunteer any further information, and Nikhil didn't ask. He wanted to approach the whole thing in a more calm and rational manner than he had hitherto—chasing after her to another city would make things worse, if anything.

Then Veena phoned. 'Nikhil, I've been trying to call Shweta but she hasn't picked up her phone. Is she all right?'

'I've no idea,' Nikhil said, his voice bleak. 'We're not engaged any more.' He waited till Veena's agitated outpourings lessened, then said, 'I don't really want to talk about it, Amma.'

'Did you fight?'

'No, we were having a wonderful time together. She just decided she didn't like the shape of my nose,' Nikhil said, his voice dripping with sarcasm. 'Of *course* we fought.'

His stepmother stayed silent long enough for Nikhil to regret his rudeness.

'I'm sorry—' he began, but Veena interrupted him.

'The fight you had with Shweta—was it something to do with your parents? Because I asked her to speak to you again. It wasn't something she would have brought up otherwise.'

'Yes, she told me that,' Nikhil said slowly. 'Why?'

'I thought she would be able to change your mind,' Veena said, sounding utterly devastated. 'I know I should have spoken to you myself, but I *had* tried, and it only made you angry.'

'It's not your fault,' Nikhil said gently. Veena in self-castigating mood could go completely out of control.

'It is. So many things are my fault—I've ruined all your lives!'

'Hang on,' Nikhil said, sounding bewildered. 'Whose lives are we talking about, here?'

There was the sound of sobbing, and then Nikhil could hear his father's voice in the background. He seemed to be trying to calm Veena down—unsuccessfully—and after a few minutes he came to the phone and said gruffly, 'Amma's too upset to talk to you now. I'll ask her to call you back when she's feeling a little better.'

Nikhil didn't reply immediately. It was a long time since he'd last spoken to his father and it felt odd to hear his voice.

'What's wrong, though? Why's she saying she's ruined my life?'

'All our lives,' his father said dryly. 'We don't agree with her, but she's going through a bad patch right now.'

Veena's voice could be heard in the background, raised in tearful and self-recriminatory protest. Nikhil could hear his own mother's soothing tones as well, and in a while Veena quietened down.

'I'm glad I've got to talk to you,' his father was saying. 'It's been a long while—the last time we spoke we both said a lot of things we didn't mean.'

'Right,' Nikhil said awkwardly.

Veena's saying that she'd ruined all their lives was making him think—Shweta had put doubts into his head already, and his father no longer seemed the villain of the piece.

'Your mother's wanted to speak to you for a long

while too,' his father said. 'But she's with your Amma right now, trying to calm her down.'

'I'll call her later,' Nikhil said. He couldn't yet bring himself to apologise for all he'd said during his last quarrel with his parents, and he knew his responses to his father sounded stilted and perhaps a little cold.

'That's all right,' his father said, and to Nikhil's surprise he added, 'Right now your priority should be making up with your young lady—from what your Amma says, she seems pretty special. And, Nikhil…?'

'Yes?' Nikhil said in neutral tones.

'Veena told Shweta a lot of things before she left Mumbai—things she's not spoken to anyone about for a long, long while. She made her swear not repeat any of it to you, but she's going to release Shweta from that promise.'

'Is this something to do with why she waited for fifteen years after I was born before she divorced you?'

'That's part of it,' Mr Nair said. 'I think it will come better from someone outside the family. All three of us have made our fair share of mistakes, and unfortunately you've been the victim of most of them.'

'Shweta and I aren't on speaking terms,' Nikhil said abruptly. 'So maybe you should tell me yourself.'

'And maybe you should try and get back on speaking terms with her,' his father said. 'If she refuses to talk to you that's different, but somehow I'm very sure she won't.'

CHAPTER TEN

THE SOUND OF a powerful car engine made Dr Mathur look up from his beloved roses. The car pulling up outside their house was black and lethal-looking, and the magnificent specimen of manhood emerging from the driver's seat looked as out of place in the little suburban street as a hawk in a chicken coop. He strode up to the little metal gate that separated the garden from the road and Dr Mathur peered up at him, suddenly feeling very old.

'Shweta's not at home,' he said. 'But you can come in.'

Nikhil hesitated. The change in Dr Mathur was disconcerting—he still remembered him as a toweringly imposing figure, and the contrast between that image and the frail, elderly man in front of him took some getting used to.

'I don't know if you remember me,' he said, hesitating a little.

Dr Mathur shot him a piercing look from under his bushy grey eyebrows. 'Nikhil Nair,' he said. 'Even if I didn't remember you I'd have guessed. Shweta's mentioned you a couple of times since she's got here. Have you had lunch?'

Nikhil shook his head. He'd left Mumbai at eleven in the morning and driven non-stop for five hours, but he was too keyed-up to think of food.

'Will Shweta be back soon?' he asked.

Dr Mathur grunted. 'I have absolutely no idea. She's gone to one of those shopping malls to get her aunt a Diwali gift.'

The disgust in his voice when he said 'shopping mall' was the kind usually reserved for words like 'cockroach farm' or 'horse manure'. Nikhil smiled involuntarily. 'Which one?'

Dr Mathur evidently thought Nikhil was clean out of his mind, going to a shopping mall to find Shweta, when he could wait in the garden for her and admire the roses instead. Still, he gave him directions to the mall, and added, 'She was planning to get some curtains as well, for the living room—though why we need new curtains I don't understand. These are perfectly OK.'

Glancing at the hideous flowery curtains at the windows, Nikhil grimaced—he could see why Shweta wanted to change them.

Shweta was wandering despondently through the mall, wishing that the Diwali decorations weren't quite so in-your-face. Not to mention the dozens of happy families milling around—it was enough to turn one's stomach. But she had managed to get her father some books he wanted, and she'd picked up a pretty cardigan for her aunt. The last 'to-do' on her list was getting a set of curtains for the living room of the Pune house.

Traditionally people spring-cleaned and painted their houses before Diwali—Dr Mathur would protest vigorously if she tried to get painters into the house, but there was little he could do about new curtains other than grumble.

She was comparing swatches of curtain fabric with a set of cushion covers when a shadow fell across the bales of cloth. 'Refusing to match, are they?' a deep voice said, and she looked up.

'What are you doing here?' she asked Nikhil ungraciously, though her legs felt so wobbly that she was glad she was already sitting down.

Nikhil surveyed her silently. She looked a little thinner, he thought, but perhaps that was his imagination. Her eyes were challenging as she looked at him, but her lips trembled slightly and he took heart from that. 'Leave these for a bit,' he said, taking her hands and pulling her to her feet. 'Let's take a walk.'

Like a marionette, Shweta found herself obediently trailing out of the store behind him. He took her hand and drew her into an almost deserted coffee shop.

'I've missed you,' he said softly. 'I can't tell you how much. Will you forgive me and come back to me?'

She was still looking at him, her eyes troubled. 'Do you still think that I…?' she began.

He was already shaking his head vigorously. 'No, I don't,' he said. 'I was being unreasonable and unfair, and… God, Shweta, I love you so much. I can't imagine what I was doing, letting you go like that.'

He was holding her by the shoulders now, rather tightly, and she gave a little gasp. 'I love you too,' she said, and then his lips came down on hers in a hot and hungry kiss.

It was a few moments before they realised where they were. Shweta emerged from his embrace with her hair tumbled and eyes glowing, took a look at the large and interested audience they had collected around them, and promptly buried her face in Nikhil's chest.

He laughed and swung her around, shielding her from the crowd with his body. 'Let's go,' he said, and they walked out of the mall, with Shweta hurrying a little to keep up with Nikhil's long strides.

Once they were in the parking lot, Nikhil took her into his arms again, kissing her unhurriedly and very, very thoroughly.

'I want us to get married as soon as possible,' Nikhil said.

Shweta nodded. She was in a state of deliciously blissful confusion—if Nikhil had suggested moving to the Andamans and living under a coconut tree she would have probably agreed just as willingly.

'Should I speak to your dad?' Nikhil asked, after another short interlude punctuated with kisses and little moans from Shweta. 'Ask him for your hand in marriage? Or do you want to tell him yourself?'

'I'll tell him myself,' Shweta said. 'Might as well do it now and get it over with. Somehow I don't think he'll be surprised.'

He wasn't.

'I suppose I should have guessed,' he said when they told him a little later. 'Well, both of you look happy, which is good. Shweta, did you remember to buy the *diyas* for Diwali?'

Shweta looked immediately guilty, but her aunt stepped in. 'That's all right—what a thing to ask the girl when she's telling you she's just got engaged! I'll go and buy the *diyas*. I'll also get some sweets and things, so that we can celebrate their engagement properly.'

'Why don't all of you come to Mumbai with me and Shweta?' Nikhil asked. 'We can celebrate Diwali there together—I was thinking of calling my family down as well.'

Dr Mathur thought it over for a while. 'Why don't you get your parents to come here instead?' he asked. 'They used to live in Pune. I'm sure they'd like to see the place again.'

'Just because you've turned into an old fuddy-duddy who hates travelling,' Shweta said, leaning over and giving her father an affectionate hug.

Nikhil's eyes widened. Shweta hadn't been lying when she'd said her relationship with her father had changed—right now it seemed as if Dr Mathur was the one in danger of being bossed around by a controlling daughter. He was even keeping his much talked-about opinions to himself.

'What do you think, Nikhil? Would they like to come?' Shweta asked. 'Diwali's more fun in a proper house than in a flat.'

The words were light, but there was an unspoken question in her eyes and he tried hard to reassure her.

'I'm sure they'd love to come—I'll call them and confirm.'

'Diwali's the day after tomorrow,' Dr Mathur said, getting to his feet. 'Better call them now and start booking tickets. Airfares will be sky-high.'

'You've started speaking to your parents again?' Shweta asked, once her father and aunt had gone indoors, tactfully leaving the two of them alone in the garden.

Nikhil nodded. 'Amma called me, but she broke down halfway through the conversation—when I told her that we'd split up. Well, from something she said I gathered that I've probably got the wrong idea about my dad, and when he took the phone I didn't start lashing into him right away.'

Shweta raised her eyebrows. 'Well, that's what's been happening the last few times we spoke,' he said.

'I'm sure he sees it as an improvement,' she said dryly. 'What did he tell you?'

'Not much, really—just that there's a reason why Amma feels she's ruining my life. And that you know what it is.' He looked Shweta squarely in the eyes. 'That's when I realised what a self-centred, bigoted idiot I've been. Even Amma confided in you rather than telling *me* what the real story is.'

'That's understandable,' Shweta said gently, and she went on to tell him what Veena had told her in Mumbai.

She kept the details of what had happened to a bare minimum, trying to focus on Nikhil's father and how he'd been if not blameless, then at least acting for what he thought was the best. Nikhil's lips tightened when she started speaking, but soon his eyes were moist.

'Don't blame Veena Aunty,' Shweta urged. 'It must

have been traumatic. She's a very private, conventional person, and the thought of you or anyone else knowing would have been unthinkable. It was only when she realised the extent of the harm she'd done you that she spoke to me.'

Nikhil shook his head. 'I'm done with blaming people,' he said. 'Poor Amma—to have carried this around with her all her life… And my poor parents too. They were trying to protect her, and into the bargain I turned against them.'

'But now you know,' Shweta said. 'And you can make it up to them.'

Nikhil's parents forgave him readily, and they were ecstatic to hear that he was about to get married. Air tickets at 'sky-high' fares were duly bought, and they along with Veena were on their way to Mumbai the next morning.

'I've hired a car to get them down to Pune,' Nikhil told Shweta. 'I could have gone and picked them up, of course, but I can't bear to let you out of my sight—I'm so worried you'll change your mind.'

'And you're even more worried you'll miss out on all the sweets Anita Bua's making,' Shweta said. 'She's spoiling you rotten—I need to speak to her.'

Nikhil shrugged and nicked a cashew from the bowl of dry fruits and nuts Shweta was chopping. 'What can I say? Women can't resist me.'

'Wait till she hears you. She'll chase you around the house with a broomstick,' Shweta said, slapping his hand away. 'Come and help me do the *rangoli*.'

Nikhil trailed out behind her, but he was more of a

hindrance than a help as Shweta used powdered colours to make the elaborate *rangoli* designs on the floor of the front veranda.

'You've got that line crooked,' he pointed out helpfully, after kissing her on the nape of the neck just as she began on the most complicated part of the design.

Shweta glared at him. 'Why don't you ask Anita Bua if she needs any help? Go and buy some more sweets or firecrackers or something.'

'Firecrackers—that's a good idea,' Nikhil said. 'I don't think anyone's bought any yet.'

He came back just as his parents arrived. His father shook hands with him formally, but both Veena and Ranjini burst into tears and threw themselves into his arms. He stood stock-still for a few seconds, then he hugged them back before pulling away.

'Shh, you'll frighten my brand-new fiancée away,' he said, smiling into their faces. It was the perfect distraction, and both women turned to exclaim over Shweta. Nikhil gave his father a wry look. 'I'm sorry,' he said softly. 'I wish you'd told me.'

Mr Nair's eyes were suspiciously damp as he clapped his son on the shoulder. 'If you'd known you'd have probably become a boring small-time builder like me,' he said. 'Look at you now—you're a hundred times more successful than you would have been if you hadn't rebelled so thoroughly.'

Later in the evening, when the older women were busy making plans for the wedding, Shweta wandered over to the corner of the porch where Nikhil had piled up the firecrackers. Because it was Diwali, and be-

cause she'd just got engaged, she'd allowed Anita Bua
to bully her into wearing a sari. The lovely pale-gold
brocade *benarasi* was draped around her slim curves
in graceful folds, and the colour set off her rather elfin
looks to perfection.

Nikhil watched her as she carefully opened one of
the packets of firecrackers. His father and future father-
in-law were discussing a rather intricate twist in state
politics. Normally he would have been interested, but
now he couldn't take his eyes off Shweta. The front
of the house was lit up with strings of fairylights, and
after she'd completed her *puja* Anita had lit the little
oil *diyas* that were placed in the *rangoli* patterns on
the porch. Shweta had now taken a candle out of one
of the packets, and was lighting it at one of the *diyas*.

'Careful!' Nikhil exclaimed, getting to his feet as
her *sari pallu* brushed the ground dangerously close
to the open flame.

Shweta gave him a teasingly provocative little smile.
'Come and help,' she said imperiously, and Nikhil went
to her side without even listening to the point Dr Mathur
was making about populism and regional vote banks.

Dr Mathur gave a rare smile as he watched Shweta.
'She reminds me so much of her mother,' he said,
and Mr Nair nodded in sympathy. He'd first met Mrs
Mathur during one of those trips to the movies, long
before Shweta was born, and the resemblance was striking.

'I shall light an *anaar* first,' Shweta was announcing. 'Actually, I shall light several. Six, I think. Line
them up in the driveway, will you?'

'Yes, ma'am,' Nikhil said.

Shweta lit a sparkler and lightly touched it to each of the *anaars*—they went up immediately, looking like a row of fiery fountains. Shweta took out a packet of rockets next. 'Ooh, I like these,' she said, and lit several of them in quick succession, her eyes following them as they shot up and exploded in a shower of multi-coloured sparks against the night sky.

Shweta's upturned face was too much of a temptation for Nikhil to resist, and he pulled her into his arms to kiss her. Shweta cast an agonised glance towards the porch, but Dr Mathur and Mr Nair were nowhere in sight. Screened from the people in the street by the rosebushes, she went willingly into Nikhil's arms.

'Do you think they'd notice if we slipped away for a bit?' Nikhil asked, nodding towards the house.

'Not until it's dinnertime,' Shweta whispered back. 'Let's light the rest of the firecrackers, and then I'll smuggle you into my room through the back door.'

'Why don't we forget the firecrackers and go now?' Nikhil muttered, bending his head to kiss her again.

Shweta gave it due consideration. 'I suppose we can,' she said. 'Make up for the week we lost.'

And that was exactly what they did.

* * * * *

ROMANCE

MEDICAL

1013 GEN STD HB

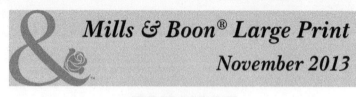

Mills & Boon® Large Print
November 2013

ROMANCE

His Most Exquisite Conquest	Emma Darcy
One Night Heir	Lucy Monroe
His Brand of Passion	Kate Hewitt
The Return of Her Past	Lindsay Armstrong
The Couple who Fooled the World	Maisey Yates
Proof of Their Sin	Dani Collins
In Petrakis's Power	Maggie Cox
A Cowboy To Come Home To	Donna Alward
How to Melt a Frozen Heart	Cara Colter
The Cattleman's Ready-Made Family	Michelle Douglas
What the Paparazzi Didn't See	Nicola Marsh

HISTORICAL

Mistress to the Marquis	Margaret McPhee
A Lady Risks All	Bronwyn Scott
Her Highland Protector	Ann Lethbridge
Lady Isobel's Champion	Carol Townend
No Role for a Gentleman	Gail Whitiker

MEDICAL

NYC Angels: Flirting with Danger	Tina Beckett
NYC Angels: Tempting Nurse Scarlet	Wendy S. Marcus
One Life Changing Moment	Lucy Clark
P.S. You're a Daddy!	Dianne Drake
Return of the Rebel Doctor	Joanna Neil
One Baby Step at a Time	Meredith Webber

Mills & Boon® Hardback
December 2013

ROMANCE

Defiant in the Desert	Sharon Kendrick
Not Just the Boss's Plaything	Caitlin Crews
Rumours on the Red Carpet	Carole Mortimer
The Change in Di Navarra's Plan	Lynn Raye Harris
The Prince She Never Knew	Kate Hewitt
His Ultimate Prize	Maya Blake
More than a Convenient Marriage?	Dani Collins
A Hunger for the Forbidden	Maisey Yates
The Reunion Lie	Lucy King
The Most Expensive Night of Her Life	Amy Andrews
Second Chance with Her Soldier	Barbara Hannay
Snowed in with the Billionaire	Caroline Anderson
Christmas at the Castle	Marion Lennox
Snowflakes and Silver Linings	Cara Colter
Beware of the Boss	Leah Ashton
Too Much of a Good Thing?	Joss Wood
After the Christmas Party...	Janice Lynn
Date with a Surgeon Prince	Meredith Webber

MEDICAL

From Venice with Love	Alison Roberts
Christmas with Her Ex	Fiona McArthur
Her Mistletoe Wish	Lucy Clark
Once Upon a Christmas Night...	Annie Claydon

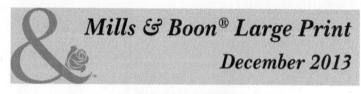

Mills & Boon® Large Print
December 2013

ROMANCE

The Billionaire's Trophy	Lynne Graham
Prince of Secrets	Lucy Monroe
A Royal Without Rules	Caitlin Crews
A Deal with Di Capua	Cathy Williams
Imprisoned by a Vow	Annie West
Duty at What Cost?	Michelle Conder
The Rings That Bind	Michelle Smart
A Marriage Made in Italy	Rebecca Winters
Miracle in Bellaroo Creek	Barbara Hannay
The Courage To Say Yes	Barbara Wallace
Last-Minute Bridesmaid	Nina Harrington

HISTORICAL

Not Just a Governess	Carole Mortimer
A Lady Dares	Bronwyn Scott
Bought for Revenge	Sarah Mallory
To Sin with a Viking	Michelle Willingham
The Black Sheep's Return	Elizabeth Beacon

MEDICAL

NYC Angels: Making the Surgeon Smile	Lynne Marshall
NYC Angels: An Explosive Reunion	Alison Roberts
The Secret in His Heart	Caroline Anderson
The ER's Newest Dad	Janice Lynn
One Night She Would Never Forget	Amy Andrews
When the Cameras Stop Rolling...	Connie Cox